Monster Allergy 2

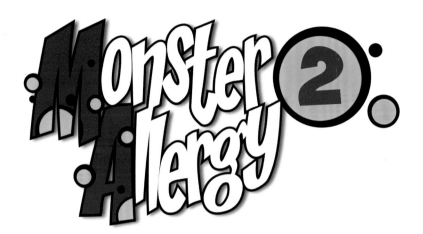

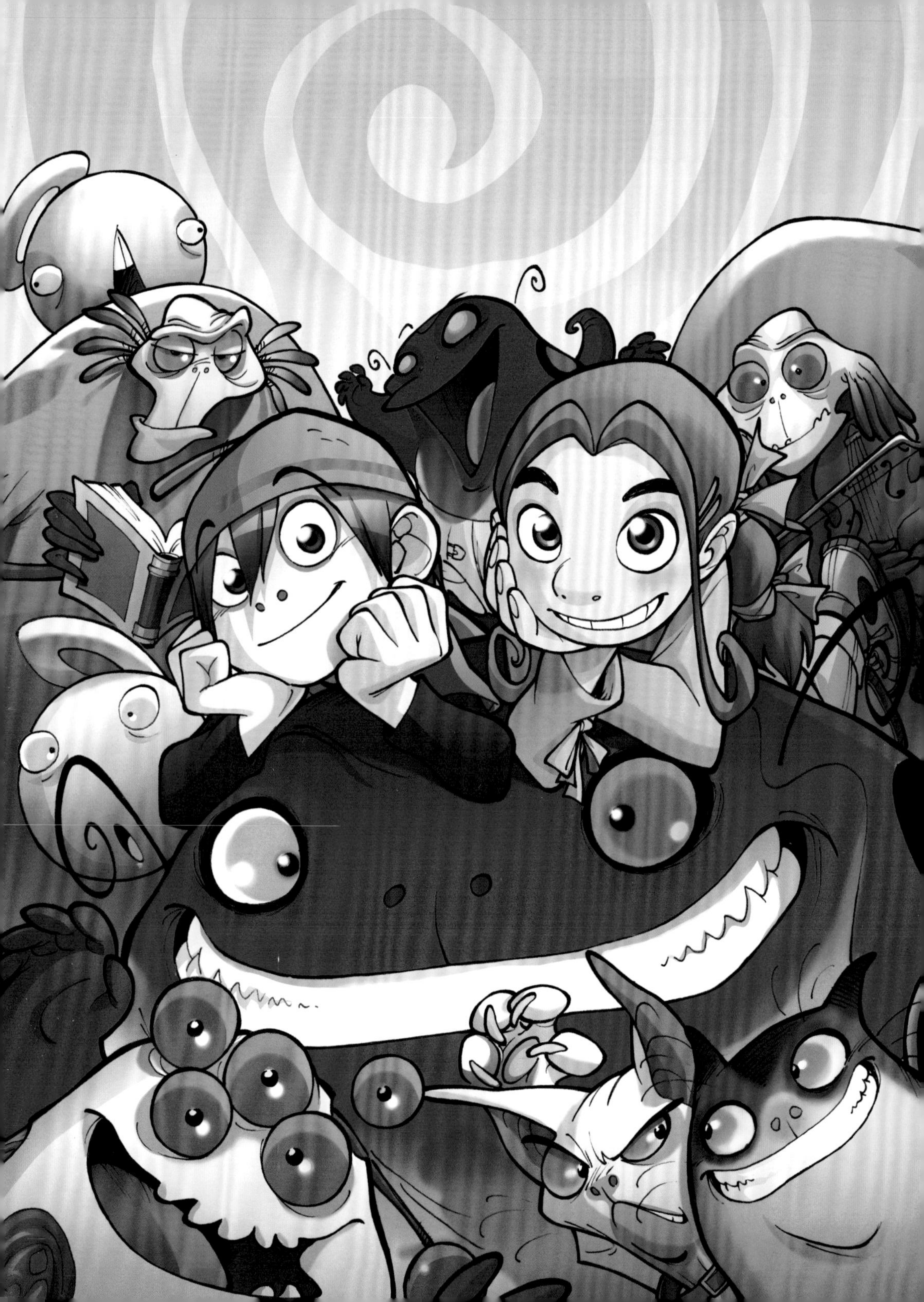

Monster Allergy 2: The Suspended City

CENTOMO • ARTIBANI • BARBUCCI • CANEPA

INSIGHT COMICS

San Rafael, California

PART 1

THE MYSTERY OF MR. MAGNACAT

Plot: Katja Centomo
Script: Francesco Artibani
Pencils: Daniela Vetro
Inks: Cristina Giorgilli
and Daniela Vetro
Design Supervisor: Alessandro Barbucci
Colors: Pamela Brughera
Colors Supervisor: Barbara Canepa

Art by Daniela Vetro and Francesco Legramandi

EARTH.

METAL.

CEMENT.

NONE OF WHAT WE FIND AROUND US IS TO OUR LIKING.

WE ARE HUNGRY.

WE HAVE BEEN STARVING FOR TOO LONG.

IT'S TIME TO EAT!

MMM...

WHAT ARE YOU DOING, DARLING?

WHAT YOU SHOULD HAVE DONE! THIS SINK HAS BEEN BLOCKED UP FOR THREE DAYS!

BUT TODAY IS SUNDAY! WE'LL CALL A PLUMBER TOMORROW. COME ON NOW...

"...IT'S TIME FOR ELENA'S SURPRISE!"

5

THIS IS FOR ME?

WHO ELSE WOULD IT BE FOR? COME ON, OPEN IT!

IT'S...A LITTLE BUNNY!

HE'S CALLED FLUFFY... BUT IF YOU DON'T LIKE THE NAME, YOU CAN CALL HIM SOMETHING ELSE.

WE KNOW HOW MUCH YOU MISS PURRCY, SO YOUR MOM AND I THOUGHT...

YOU THOUGHT YOU'D REPLACE HIM! WELL, YOU THOUGHT WRONG! PURRCY ISN'T DEAD. HE GOT CATNAPPED AND I'M GONNA FIND HIM!

LOOK HOW CUTE HE IS! HE ALREADY LIKES YOU!

HE'S NOT A CAT, MOM!

IT WOULD NEVER BE THE SAME!

WHY NOT? HE'S GOT WHISKERS, HE'S FURRY, AND HE EATS A LOT!

WELL, SO DOES UNCLE RONNIE! BUT HE ISN'T A CAT EITHER!

THAT REMINDS ME... YOUR BROTHER IS COMING BY TO PICK UP PORTER LATER THIS EVENING.

SURE, NO PROBLEM.

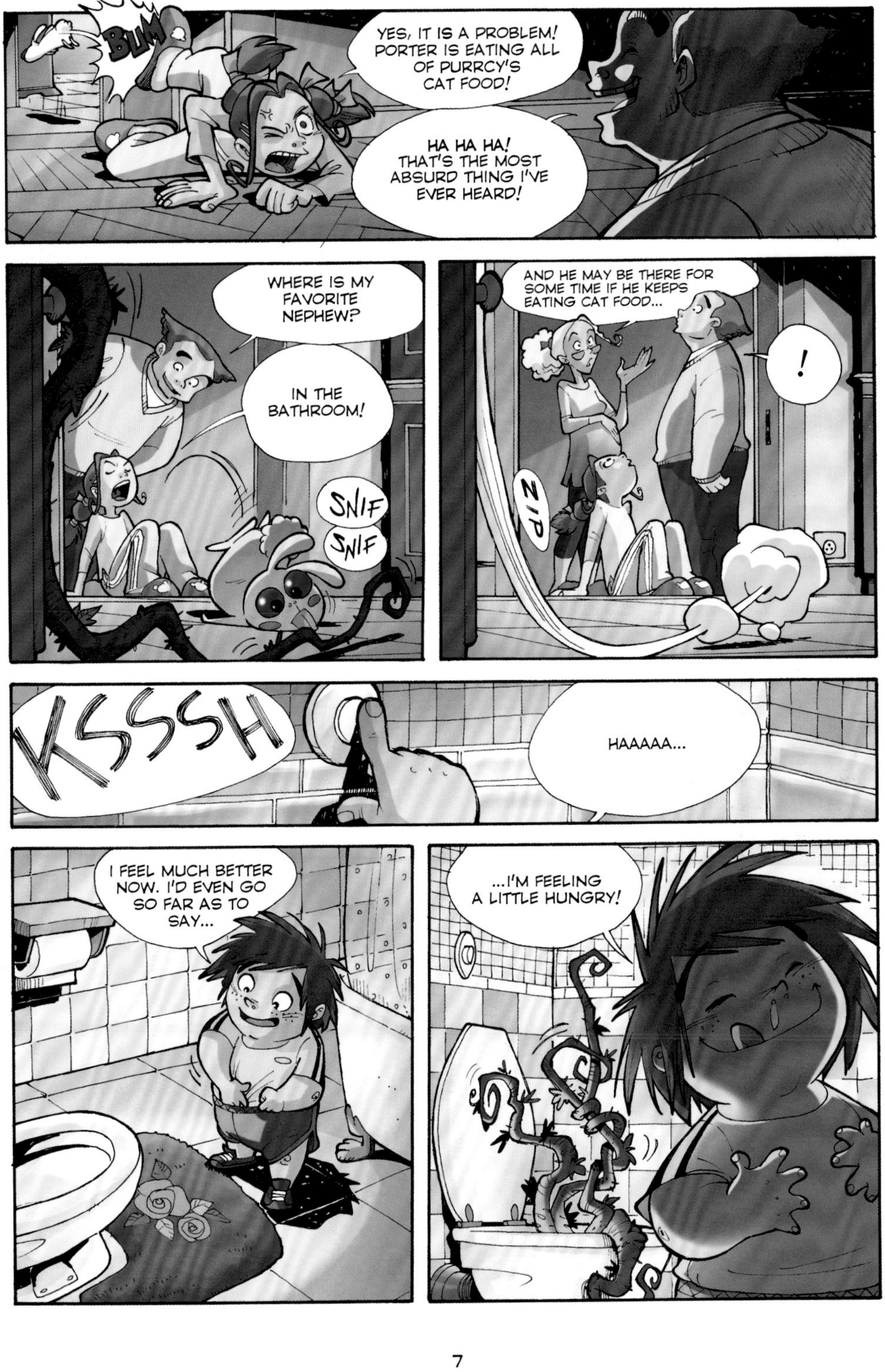
BUM
YES, IT IS A PROBLEM! PORTER IS EATING ALL OF PURRCY'S CAT FOOD!
HA HA HA! THAT'S THE MOST ABSURD THING I'VE EVER HEARD!
WHERE IS MY FAVORITE NEPHEW?
IN THE BATHROOM!
SNIF
SNIF
AND HE MAY BE THERE FOR SOME TIME IF HE KEEPS EATING CAT FOOD...
!
ZIP
KSSSH
HAAAAA...
I FEEL MUCH BETTER NOW. I'D EVEN GO SO FAR AS TO SAY...
...I'M FEELING A LITTLE HUNGRY!

SUNDAYS ARE UNLIKE ANY OTHER DAY IN BIGBURG...

...AND THIS PARTICULAR ONE, DOWN IN OLDMILL...

PLOP

PLOP

...WOULD BE A VERY SPECIAL SUNDAY INDEED FOR A CERTAIN SOMEONE.

WE'RE GOING FOR A LITTLE WALK, ELENA. ARE YOU SURE YOU DON'T WANT TO COME ALONG?

ONE HUNDRED PERCENT SURE! HAVE FUN!

I THINK THEY'RE UPSET ABOUT THE WHOLE RABBIT THING. MAYBE I WAS A BIT HARSH!

BUT I TOLD THEM THE TRUTH! EVEN IF THAT FUR-BALL IS CUTE...HE'S NOT PURRCY!

HEY, ELENA...

...LOOK WHAT I FOUND!

AAAAAH!

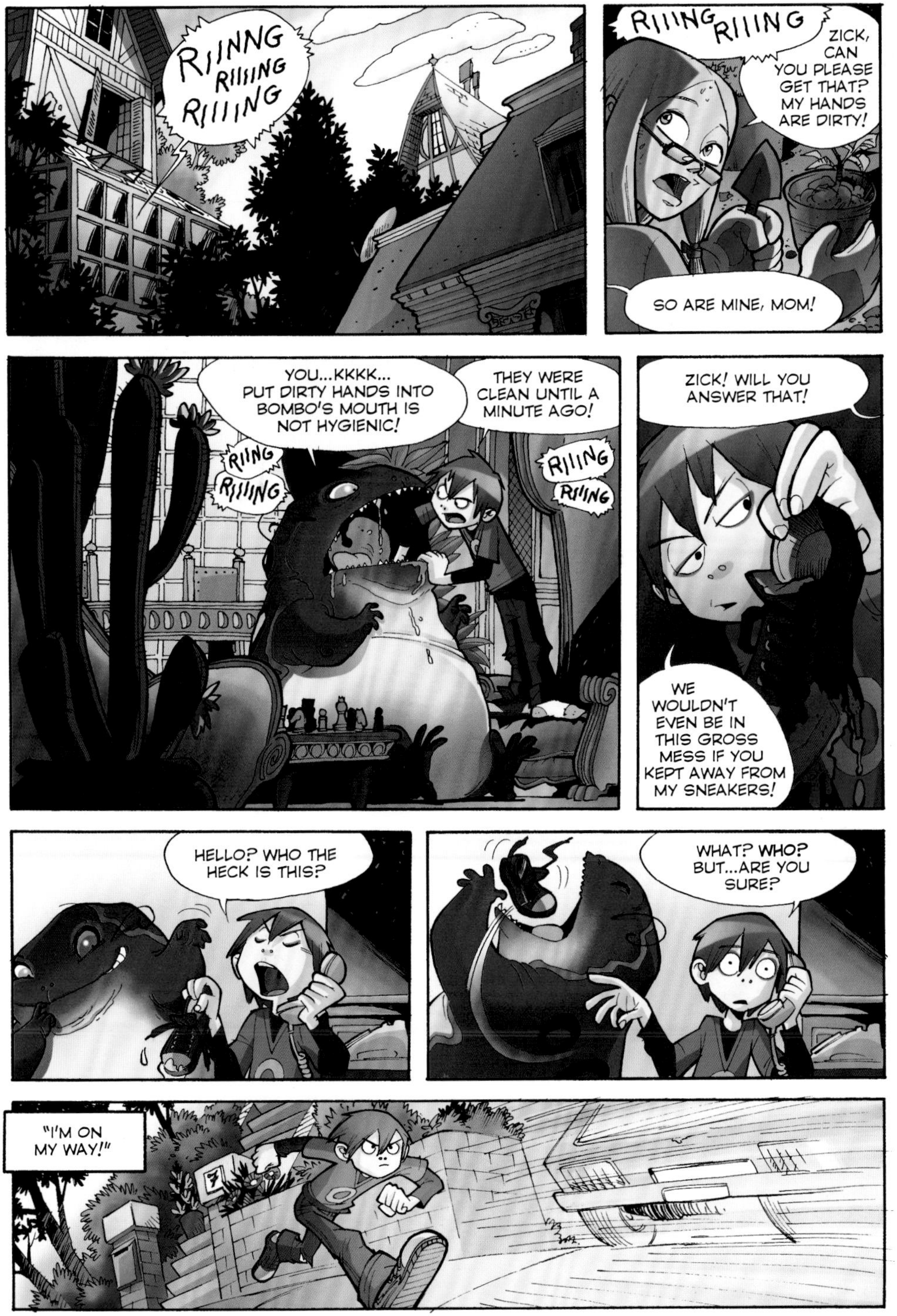

RIIINNG RIIIING RIIIING
RIIIING RIIIING
ZICK, CAN YOU PLEASE GET THAT? MY HANDS ARE DIRTY!
SO ARE MINE, MOM!
YOU...KKKK... PUT DIRTY HANDS INTO BOMBO'S MOUTH IS NOT HYGIENIC!
THEY WERE CLEAN UNTIL A MINUTE AGO!
RIIING RIIIING
RIIIING RIIING
ZICK! WILL YOU ANSWER THAT!
WE WOULDN'T EVEN BE IN THIS GROSS MESS IF YOU KEPT AWAY FROM MY SNEAKERS!
HELLO? WHO THE HECK IS THIS?
WHAT? WHO? BUT...ARE YOU SURE?
"I'M ON MY WAY!"

I...I DON'T KNOW WHAT HAPPENED TO THEM! THEY JUST SHOWED UP ALL OF A SUDDEN...

!

...AND THEY LOOKED LIKE THIS!

LIKE WHAT?

LOOK AT THOSE FACES! THEY KEEP MOVING AROUND!

AH...AH... ATCH...

CAN YOU HEAR ME IF I MOVE MY MOUTH UP HERE?

ATCHOOOM!

HEY! WHY DON'T YOU COVER YOUR NOSE WHEN YOU SNEEZE?

KFFF

KFFF

KFFF

WHAT'S GOING ON, ZICK?

NOTHING GOOD... I CAN FEEL A DANGEROUS PRESENCE! BUT NOT ONLY IN THIS ROOM...

...IT'S IN THE WHOLE HOUSE!

HOLY SPIT! WHAT CAN WE DO? IF MY PARENTS GET BACK AND SEE PORTER LIKE THIS, THEY'LL SKIN ME ALIVE!

WOULD THEY REALLY DO THAT?

NO...BUT THIS WOULD GIVE THEM THE PERFECT OPPORTUNITY!

BUT IT'S NOT YOUR FAULT!

SURE, BUT WHOSE IS IT?

THAT'S WHAT I'M GONNA FIND OUT! YOU KEEP AN EYE ON THEM. I'LL TAKE CARE OF THE REST...

MY MONSTERITIS IS NEVER WRONG, SO I'M ONLY GOING TO ASK YOU THIS ONCE...

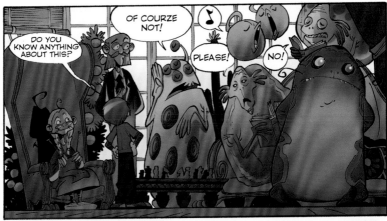

DO YOU KNOW ANYTHING ABOUT THIS?

OF COURZE NOT!

PLEASE!

NO!

AND YOU, BOMBO?

ME... ME...

BOMBO SO SORRY, ZICK! WAAAAAAH!

WHAT AN IDIOT!

WE ONLY TRY TO SCARE GIRL! IT WAS A JOKE!

EXACTLY! THE MONSTER POD WORRIES YOU, BUT IT WON'T BURY YOU!

THE MONSTER POD? YOU RELEASED THE MONSTER POD?

COME ON, THERE'S NO NEED TO MAKE SUCH A FUSS OUT OF IT!

CAN...CAN YOU EXPLAIN WHAT YOU'RE TALKING ABOUT?

THESE TWERPS HAVE UNLEASHED A DIGESTING PLANT ON YOUR FRIEND!

WE ONLY WANTED TO SHAKE UP THE LITTLE SNOT-NOSE'S MONSTEROSAS!

BUT HUMAN BEINGS AREN'T LIKE YOU! WE DON'T HAVE MONSTEROSAS! WE HAVE BONES! FLESH! MUSCLES!

BUT YOU TWO, FOR EXAMPLE...

WE'RE GHOSTS! DEAD HUMANS!

SPEAK FOR YOURSELF! I'VE NEVER FELT BETTER IN MY LIFE!

GRANDMA, WHAT ARE MONSTEROSAS?

WHAT A MESS! WHAT A MESS!

IT'S WHAT MONSTERS ARE MADE OF! THEY'RE A BIT LIKE CELLS... BUT UGLIER!

TONS OF HORRIBLE TINY BRICKS THAT, WHEN ASSEMBLED, GIVE YOU WORKS OF ART LIKE THESE GUYS.

OKAY! MAYBE VE DID VRONG... BUT ZAT EES NO REASON TO INSULT US!

ZICK BE ANGRY WITH BOMBO?

OH, NO! ZICK IS ANGRY WITH EVERYONE!

MONSTEROSAS! DIGESTING PLANTS! WHY AM I ALWAYS THE LAST TO KNOW ABOUT THESE THINGS?

THAT'S NOT TRUE! YOU KNOW THAT WE DON'T KEEP SECRETS FROM YOU!

SO WHY DIDN'T ANYONE EVER TELL ME ABOUT THE SUSPENDED CITY OVER BIGBURG?*

BECAUSE YOU NEVER ASKED US ABOUT IT!

*SEE MONSTER ALLERGY, VOL. 1

IT'S CALLED BIBBUR-SI, MY BOY...

"...AND IT'S THE CITY OF MONSTERS!"

SUCH HOSPITALITY! THEY REALLY MAKE YOU FEEL AT HOME HERE...

...PROVIDED THAT YOU LIVE IN A SEWER!

IF I WERE YOU I'D BE LESS FUSSY...

...BECAUSE THIS MESS WILL SAVE OUR SKIN, AT LEAST FOR A LITTLE WHILE, KITTY!

I'VE ALREADY TOLD YOU NOT TO CALL ME KITTY!

SO WHAT WOULD YOU LIKE ME TO CALL YOU? MOUSE?

I EXPECT TO BE RESPECTED! I AM A TUTOR!

SO WHAT? I'M A TUTOR, TOO.

BUT I'M FIRST RANK!

FWAN

WHAT A COINCIDENCE! I'M FIRST RANK, TOO.

WELL, I'M... I'M SUPERIOR FIRST RANK!

HMPH! I DIDN'T KNOW THAT WAS A RANK...

WELL, IT IS! NOW THAT WE'VE ESTABLISHED WHO'S WHO, SHALL WE TRY TO FIGURE OUT A PLAN TO GET OUT OF HERE?

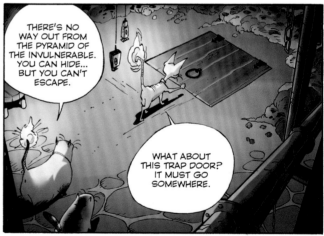

THERE'S NO WAY OUT FROM THE PYRAMID OF THE INVULNERABLE. YOU CAN HIDE... BUT YOU CAN'T ESCAPE.

WHAT ABOUT THIS TRAP DOOR? IT MUST GO SOMEWHERE.

THAT'S WHERE THE CATS GO AFTER THEY'VE MET THE BARBER...

COME TO THINK OF IT, I'M NOT REALLY THAT CURIOUS TO FIND OUT WHAT'S BEHIND IT.

SOMEONE KNOWS OUR SECRET, TIMOTHY...

...AND FOR SOME REASON HE'S LOOKING FOR US.

!

KLANK
KLANK

THE BARBER IS COMING BACK! EVERYONE, HIDE!

!

ZOMP

ZOMP

TUMP

TUMP

WHAT SORT OF A NIGHTMARE HAVE I GOT MYSELF INTO? I'VE FAILED IN MY DUTY TO SAVE THE FLEABAG...

BZZZEEEEE

...AND NOW WHO'S GOING TO SAVE ME?!

MEEEEOW!!

WHERE ARE YOU GOING, ZICK?

I'M JUST GOING DOWN TO THE BASEMENT FOR A SEC, MOM.

DON'T FORGET YOUR *INHALER!* IT'S REALLY DUSTY DOWN THERE.

DON'T WORRY!

AND WHEN YOU COME BACK UP, BRING A JAR OF JAM WITH YOU!

JAM! MMMM...

AND WHAT DO YOU THINK IS DOWN HERE?

A DIGESTING PLANT IS A NASTY PIECE OF WORK... BUT WE'LL NEED TO GET UP CLOSE TO TELL HOW BAD IT IS!

THE OLDMILL NEIGHBORHOOD IS A GHOST DISTRICT, THE WORST SORT OF GROUND TO PLANT A MONSTER POD!

WHAT'S A GHOST DISTRICT, GRANDPA?

LET'S JUST SAY... IT'S A PLACE WHERE MONSTERS ARE SENT FOR PUNISHMENT!

AND WHAT DID THEY DO TO END UP BEING PUNISHED?

NOTHING THAT SERIOUS, FOR US HUMANS, THAT IS...

HOWEVER, WHATEVER THEY DID, THEY HAVE TO LEARN NOT TO DO IT ANYMORE.

THE MONSTER POD JOKE WILL LENGTHEN THE STAY OF THESE SMART FELLOWS!

OUR BASEMENT BORDERS THE NEIGHBORS' BASEMENT! WE'LL SEE IMMEDIATELY WHETHER THE PLANT HAS SPREAD. OPEN THE DOOR!

IT'S LOCKED!

THE KEY, BOMBO!

GLIP

TRAK TRAK

TRAK

ATCHOO!

!

!

WH... WHAT'S IN THERE?

OH... UM... NOTHING IMPORTANT, BOY! THAT FOOL BOMBO JUST GAVE ME THE WRONG KEY!

SLAM

I WANTED THE OTHER KEY! YOU CAN GET RID OF THIS ONE!

GLIP

I REALLY HOPE YOU CHOKE!

GLOM

TRAK

TRAK

TRAK

RIGHT, LET'S HAVE A LOOK HERE...

!

BUT A SECOND AGO THERE WAS...

...THE SAME STUFF THAT THERE IS NOW! THE SHADOWS CREATE STRANGE ILLUSIONS SOMETIMES--THEY MAKE YOU SEE THINGS THAT AREN'T THERE!

NO TRACE OF THE DIGESTING PLANT. IT KNOWS TO KEEP AWAY FROM HERE.

BUT IT'S NOT FAR, GRANDPA! MY NOSE IS ITCHING MORE AND MORE...AND... AND...

ATCHOO!

BE CAREFUL! IT'S BEHIND THIS WALL!

HMM...

SNAP

CHOMP

CRUNCH

CHOMP

WHAT'S GOING ON? GRANDPA! SAY SOMETHING!

I'M TELLING YOU THAT THIS IS ONE HECK OF A BRAINTEASER, ZICK!

!

AAAAA-AARGH!

THE MONSTER POD IS UNDERNEATH YOUR FRIEND'S HOUSE, BUT IT HASN'T STOPPED THERE!

POP!

IT'S GONE DOWN EVEN DEEPER THAN THAT... BEFORE LONG THAT PLANT WILL START EATING OLDMILL FROM THE FOUNDATIONS UP!

THAT'S HORRIBLE! WHAT... WHAT DO WE DO?

ME HAVE IDEA! LET'S MAKE IT SHRIVEL UP!

THANK YOU, BOMBO! YOU CAN LEAVE YOUR SUGGESTION IN THE TRASH ON YOUR WAY OUT!

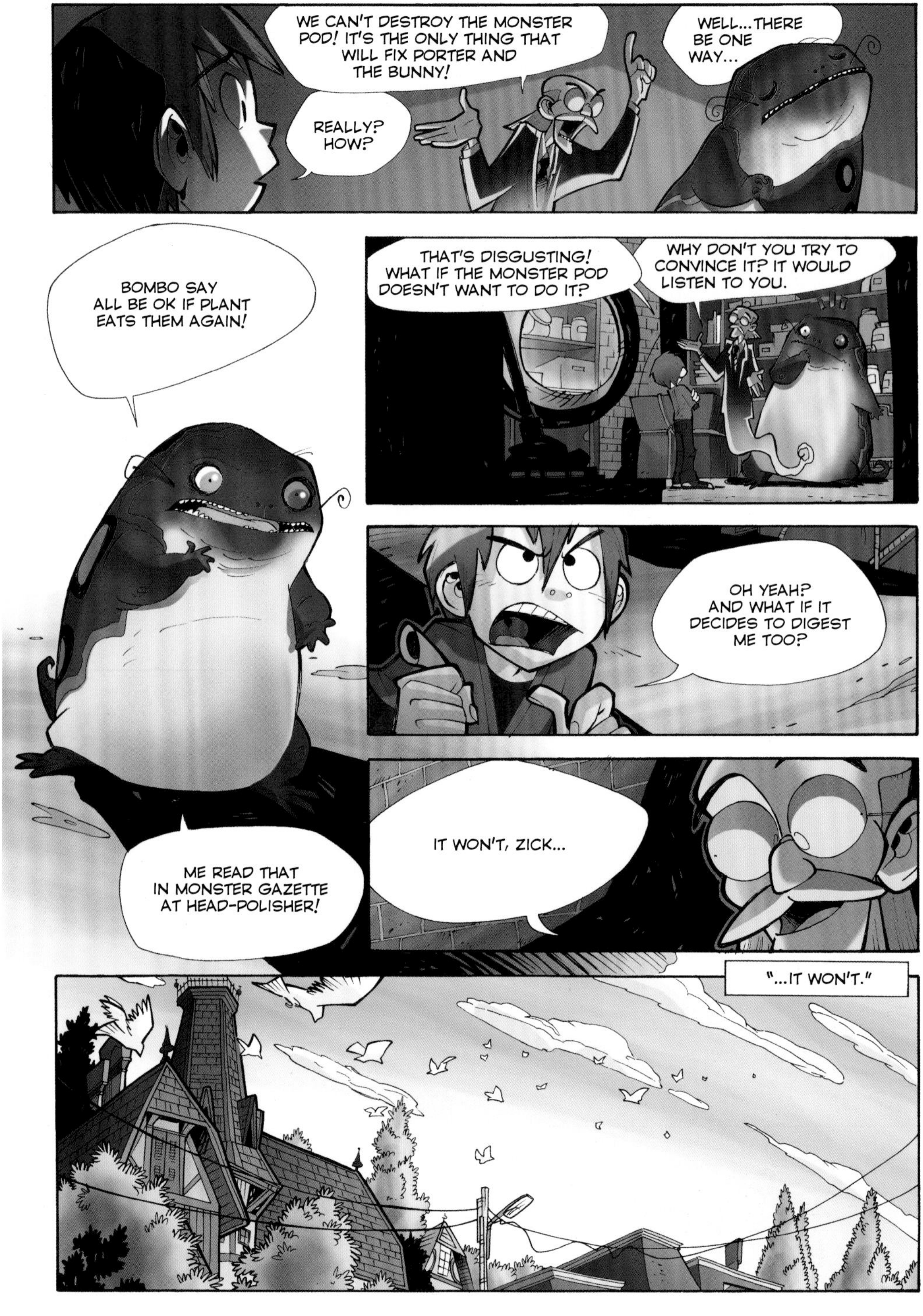

WE CAN'T DESTROY THE MONSTER POD! IT'S THE ONLY THING THAT WILL FIX PORTER AND THE BUNNY!
REALLY? HOW?
WELL...THERE BE ONE WAY...
BOMBO SAY ALL BE OK IF PLANT EATS THEM AGAIN!
THAT'S DISGUSTING! WHAT IF THE MONSTER POD DOESN'T WANT TO DO IT?
WHY DON'T YOU TRY TO CONVINCE IT? IT WOULD LISTEN TO YOU.
OH YEAH? AND WHAT IF IT DECIDES TO DIGEST ME TOO?
ME READ THAT IN MONSTER GAZETTE AT HEAD-POLISHER!
IT WON'T, ZICK...
"...IT WON'T."

YOU NEED TO HURRY UP AND DECIDE, BECAUSE WE DON'T HAVE MUCH TIME! YOUR PARENTS COULD COME BACK ANY SECOND!

I...I DON'T KNOW WHAT TO DO!

LET'S VOTE! WHO'S WITH ME?

ME!

TWO TO ONE! THE RABBIT DOESN'T COUNT. YOU'RE COMING WITH US, ELENA!

HOLY SPIT! IT'S EASY TO WIN LIKE THAT! PORTER NEVER SAYS NO TO GETTING DIRTY.

WHAT AM I GOING TO SAY TO MY UNCLE AND AUNT IF I LOSE HIM IN THE SEWER?!

LISTEN, THE IDEA OF GOING DOWN THERE DOESN'T APPEAL TO ME EITHER, BUT WE DON'T HAVE A CHOICE!

WILL THEY MAKE IT?

I'M SURE OF IT, BOMBO! ZICK DOESN'T KNOW IT YET... BUT HE HAS GREAT POWERS.

GRIIIIND

NO ONE AROUND. THE COAST IS CLEAR!

DON'T PUSH!

CLUNG

HMM...

21

I HOPE FOR YOUR SAKE THAT THIS MIRACULOUS PLANT REALLY DOES EXIST! IF I FIND OUT THAT YOU MADE ME GET MY NEW SHOES DIRTY FOR NOTHING, I'LL MAKE YOU PAY!

THEY'RE NOT NEW! YOU'VE HAD THEM FOR A WEEK!

HEY! SO YOU'RE KEEPING TRACK OF ME NOW?

CRIPES, ELENA, PUT THAT FLASHLIGHT DOWN!

DON'T SHINE IT IN MY EYES! KEEP IT IN FRONT OF YOU! THERE'S SOMETHING VERY DANGEROUS AROUND HERE!

STAY HERE AND KEEP YOUR EYES OPEN!

WHY CAN'T I COME? IF THERE'S A MONSTROUS PLANT THEN I WANT TO SEE IT TOO!

ABSOLUTELY NOT! PORTER, FLUFFY, AND I ARE GOING. IF SOMETHING HAPPENS TO US, THEN GO BACK AND GET HELP!

AND IF SOMETHING HAPPENS TO ME?

WE'LL WORRY ABOUT THAT IF IT HAPPENS!

DON'T FALL IN THE WATER, ZICK! IT WOULD BE HARD TO TELL YOU APART FROM ALL THAT POOP!

IS IT FAR, ZICK?

NO, PORTER...

ATCHOO!

...WE'RE HERE!

22

D-DON'T MOVE, PORTER!

WHY?

PUFF FFF!

UFF!

WELL, WHADDA-YAKNOW? THE BOY CAN SEE US!

WHAT FUN! HE MIGHT BE TASTY, TOO!

YOU'RE NOT THINKING OF EATING ME, RIGHT? GRANDPA SAID YOU'D BE FULL!

US? FULL? HA HA HA!

A MONSTER POD IS NEVER FULL...

...AND EVEN WHEN WE'VE EATEN THIS ENTIRE TOWN, WE'LL STILL HAVE A LITTLE BIT OF ROOM LEFT IN OUR STOMACH!

ZWAP

RUN!

WE'RE NOT INTERESTED IN THEM! WE'VE ALREADY TASTED THEM!

YEOW!

WE WANT YOU!

THAT SOUNDED LIKE ZICK!

THERE'S NO USE RUNNING, SNOT-NOSE...

...BECAUSE WE'RE EVERYWHERE!

WHAT'S GOING ON? WHERE IS ZICK?

I DON'T KNOW! HE STARTED TALKING TO HIMSELF AND THEN HE RAN FOR IT! YOUR FRIEND IS WEIRD!

TCHACK

AH!

BDUMP

DON'T RUN, KIDDO!

YEAH! THERE'S NOTHING WORSE THAN A SWEATY SNACK!

THUD

ACCEPT IT! THIS IS THE END FOR YOU!

YOU SHOULD'NT HAVE COME DOWN HERE.

THIS IS OUR KINGDOM NOW...

AND YOU ARE TRESPAS- SING!

ZICK?

IS EVERYTHING ALRIGHT?

AHA! WE'RE INVISIBLE TO HER!

IT'LL BE FUN TO SWALLOW HER WHOLE!

WHAT ARE YOU DOING HERE? I TOLD YOU NOT TO MOVE!

DON'T COME CLOSER!

I AM COMING CLOSER! I CAN'T KICK YOU FROM BACK HERE!

HERE I AM, WORRIED ABOUT YOU AND THIS IS HOW YOU THANK ME?

OH NO...

KEEP. AWAY.

ARE YOU CRAZY?

Y...YOU USED THE TONE!

AND WE MUST OBEY! WE...WE CAN'T RESIST!

Y...YOU ARE A LITTLE TAMER!

UH?

I'LL ASK YOU AGAIN, ZICK! IS EVERY-THING OK?

WHAT DID YOU CALL ME?

CRAZY!

LITTLE TAMER...

YOU ALWAYS USE...UNFAIR METHODS!

MAY YOU BE DAMNED!

WHAT ELSE...WHAT ELSE WOULD YOU LIKE US TO DO?

I WANT YOU TO MAKE MY FRIENDS WHOLE AGAIN! DIGEST THEM. AGAIN.

BUT HE'S REVOLT-ING...

MAYBE SO... BUT I USED THE TONE!

WHO ARE YOU TALKING TO?

ARRGH RAAA!

MAYBE... ARE THERE MONSTERS AROUND HERE, ZICK? HUH? ARE THERE MONSTERS?

PLEASE ELENA! NOT NOW!

HOLY SPIT! THEY'VE DISAPPEARED!

REALLY?

CRUNCH

CRUNCH

CRUNCH

BUT THEY'RE HERE, RIGHT IN FRONT OF YOU!

BLORCH

B-BUT... BUT... THAT'S IMPOSSIBLE!

COOL! CAN WE DO THAT AGAIN?

NOW LET'S GET OUT OF HERE...

AT LEAST LEAVE US THE RABBIT, LITTLE TAMER! EVEN A FINGER OF THE GIRL WOULD BE FINE!

WE'RE SO HUNGRY...

I'LL THROW A CHEESE SANDWICH DOWN THE TOILET FOR YOU! YOU'D DO WELL TO MAKE IT LAST!

Rrrr...

AS YOU WISH...

YOU'RE IN CHARGE...

...LITTLE TAMER!

IN BIGBURG, BARBERS DON'T WORK ON SUNDAY...

...BUT THIS BARBER NEVER HAS A DAY OFF...

MEOOOW!

BzeeEEE

Bzeeeee

...BECAUSE IN CAT PRISON THERE'S ALWAYS SOMEONE WAITING TO BE SERVED.

GOOD HEAVENS, WHAT A SIGHT!

YOU'RE RIGHT! SO YOUNG... AND ALREADY SO COVERED IN WRINKLES!

YOU'RE ONE TO TALK! WHAT ABOUT YOUR WRINKLES?

THEY'RE NOT WRINKLES! THEY ARE CHARACTER LINES!

HUH?

OOF!

YOU IDIOT...

IN YOU GO, SWEET-HEART!

MeEeo

MaAaaOW

Rrrr...

Maaaow

MeEeOW

MAAAAO

RRR..

RRRR..

FTUP!

ONE MORE DOWN THE CHUTE...

AND NOW LET'S SEE WHAT'S GOING ON HERE!

!

THE ANSWER IS **NO**, ZICK! JUST FORGET IT! THE FIRST CAT THAT DISAPPEARED WAS MINE...

...AND YOU'RE NOT GOING ANYWHERE WITHOUT ME! IF WE'RE GOING TO WORK TOGETHER THEN WE NEED TO AGREE!

AND WHO SAID WE'RE GOING TO WORK TOGETHER?

IT'S BETTER IF YOU KEEP OUT OF IT THIS TIME! PURRCY AND TIMOTHY WERE CATNAPPED BY REALLY DANGEROUS PEOPLE!

HOW DANGEROUS? WHY DON'T YOU TELL ME WHAT YOU SAW?

NO- THING, I TOLD YOU...

I CAN'T STAND THIS! YOU CAN'T TREAT ME LIKE THIS!

IF CHARLIE SCHUSTER WERE HERE, WE WOULD HAVE ALREADY FOUND PURRCY!

AND WHO IS THIS CHARLIE SCHUSTER?

HE'S MY BEST FRIEND, ZICK! WE HAVE **NO** SECRETS!

NOW YOU CAN GO, IF YOU WANT TO! NO ONE'S STOPPING YOU!

AHEM... DO YOU HAVE A PLAN, OR ARE WE GOING TO IMPROVISE?

HMM... THE SALESMAN'S VISITING CARD AND THE GUIDE TO THE PYRAMID OF THE INVULNERABLE!

THAT'S NOT MUCH TO GO BY. AND THEY'RE NOTHING NEW.

LET'S BREAK THE GUIDE IN HALF!

THERE COULD BE A MAP OR A PHOTO OF PUNZO IN HIS UNDERWEAR IN THE BINDING!

THAT'S THE WAY IT ALWAYS WORKS IN COMICS.

OH YEAH? AND WHAT COMICS DO YOU READ?

"GHOST MAN"! IT'S SO COOL!

HMM...

CAN I LOOK AT THE CARD? I'LL GIVE IT RIGHT BACK.

GNAW! SNARL!

YIKES!

SINCE THE PLANT SWALLOWED HIM, HE'S BEEN A BIT TENSE...

WHAT ARE YOU GOING TO DO WITH IT?

DO YOU SEE THIS SLOT? IT'S JUST AN IDEA, BUT...

TLICK

...BUT IT MIGHT JUST WORK!

HOLY SPIT!

ZWiii'N

GLORY AND HONOR TO MAGNACAT, BROTHERS AND SISTERS!

WELCOME TO THE PYRAMID OF THE INVULNERABLE!

YOU'RE ALWAYS WELCOME IN THIS HOUSE... AND THE DOORS ARE ALWAYS OPEN TO YOU!

DID YOU HEAR THAT ZICK?

"IF THAT ISN'T AN INVITATION..."

SO? CAN YOU SEE ANYTHING?

I CAN SEE THE SAME THINGS AS YOU! A KITCHEN STORE WITH PEOPLE SELLING POTS AND PANS!

KFFF KFFF KFFF

AND NOW?

LET'S HAVE A LOOK THROUGH THERE. BUT TRY TO BE DISCREET!

AND WHERE DO YOU THINK YOU'RE GOING, CHILDREN?

WE...GASP! WE...

WE WANTED TO HAVE A LOOK AROUND!

IT SAYS HERE THAT YOUR DOORS ARE ALWAYS OPEN!

KFFF KFFF

OH! OF COURSE! I...I DIDN'T KNOW! THIS WAY, PLEASE!

HE WAS ONE OF THEM, WASN'T HE? I COULD TELL FROM YOUR FACE.

WE AGREED TO BE DISCREET, DANG IT!

OH, SHUT UP! WE'RE INSIDE NOW...AND THAT'S ALL THAT MATTERS.

31

IF THERE WERE A MAP OF THIS DUMP IN HERE, WE'D KNOW WHERE WE NEED TO GO!

FRUSH FRUSH

MAYBE SOMETHING LIKE THIS!

YOU ARE HERE

LIFT LIFT LIFT LIFT

WHEN WE MOVE, THE LITTLE DOT MOVES WITH US!

TLING

WOW! THIS MUST BE OUR LUCKY DAY...

YOU!

...OR MAYBE NOT!

VLADIMIR PUNZO!

SO, YOU REMEMBER ME, YOU LITTLE BUSYBODIES! WHAT ARE YOU DOING HERE? HOW DID YOU GET INSIDE?

WE... WE...

SAVE YOUR BREATH! YOU CAN TELL YOUR STORY DIRECTLY TO MR. MAGNACAT!

AAAAH!

TO THE TOP OF THE PYRAMID, FRITZ! AND MAKE IT SNAPPY!

YES, SIR!

ATCHOO!

ATCHOO!

ARE YOU OK, ZICK?

OH... SOON HE'LL BE FEELING MUCH WORSE!

YOU BRATS HAVE MESSED WITH THE WRONG PEOPLE! YOU TRICKED ME AND THEN YOU STOLE SOMETHING OF MINE!

COFF!

COFF!

WE'RE HERE...

KFFF

KFFF

GLORY AND HONOR TO MAGNA-CAT!

NOW AND FOREVER, FRITZ...

...NOW AND FOREVER!

SUPREME LORD! I KNEEL IN THE PRESENCE OF YOUR GREATNESS!

ZICK, I'M SCARED!

RISE, VLADIMIR...

...CAN'T YOU SEE YOU'RE FRIGHTENING OUR GUESTS?

IS SOMETHING WRONG, MY LITTLE FRIEND?

I... I...

AAAAH NNN...

ZICK!

HAH! THIS BOY...

HE'S THE NOSY BRAT I WAS TELLING YOU ABOUT, SIR! I CAUGHT HIM AND THE GIRL WANDERING AROUND THE HALL.

TAKE THIS, MY BOY! A GLASS OF WATER WILL DO YOU GOOD.

IT'S...OK! I'M BETTER NOW, THANK YOU!

WHY ARE YOU THANKING HIM? HAVE YOU FORGOTTEN WHY WE'RE HERE?

RIGHT. TO WHAT DO I OWE THIS VISIT?

LET'S MAKE IT SHORT, MISTER! GIVE US BACK OUR CATS! HE STOLE THEM, AND NOW WE WANT THEM BACK!

CATS? WHAT IS SHE TALKING ABOUT, VLADIMIR?

DON'T TRY AND BE CLEVER WITH US! THERE'S TONS OF WEIRD STUFF GOING ON IN HERE, WHAT WITH THE PYRAMID OF THE INTOLERABLE AND ALL THAT...

...OF THE INVULNERABLE, PLEASE!

AHA! SO IT'S TRUE!

PLEASE, LEAVE US, VLADIMIR.

YOU KNOW, SWEETIE... I WISH YOUR STORIES WERE TRUE! MY WORK WOULD BE MUCH MORE FUN!

I'D HAVE A MYSTERY TO INVESTIGATE... BUT UNFORTUNATELY EVERYTHING IN THIS BUILDING IS COMPLETELY NORMAL.

THEN HOW DO YOU EXPLAIN THE WEIRD SECRET MESSAGES?

THAT'S SIMPLY HOW WE DO BUSINESS, MY DEAR.

I'M JUST THE PRESIDENT OF A COMPANY THAT MAKES EXCELLENT POTS...

...AND YOU'RE A LITTLE GIRL WITH AN EXTRAORDINARY IMAGINATION.

IF YOU ONLY KNEW HOW I ENVY YOU!

CAN WE...CAN WE GO NOW?

SURE! I'D ASK YOU TO LUNCH, BUT I ALREADY HAVE PLANS.

LET'S GO, ELENA! DON'T STOP UNTIL WE'RE OUT OF HERE!

COME BACK WHENEVER YOU LIKE... AND REMEMBER THAT MR. MAGNACAT HAS NOTHING TO HIDE!

I AM JUST AS I APPEAR TO BE!

I'M QUITE TRANSPARENT!

"AND I LOVE CATS!"

WHY DID YOU LET THEM GO, SIR? THAT GIRL IS A MEDDLING SCHEMER!

BUT THE BOY IS AN INTERESTING ONE. I COULD HARDLY BEAR HAVING HIM NEAR ME.

THAT BOY IS MORE THAN HE APPEARS TO BE, VLADIMIR!

I WANT TO KNOW WHAT YOU SAW THIS TIME.

I SAW A MONSTER, ELENA! THE UGLIEST OF THEM ALL...

I SAW MAGNA-CAT.

AND NOW I KNOW WHAT I NEED TO DO!

AHA! NOW YOU'RE TALKING!

TO RESCUE PURRCY AND TIMOTHY, WE NEED TO GET IN FROM BELOW! THE BASE-MENT OF THAT BUILDING IS ENORMOUS!

AND THIS TIME, WE'LL GET REINFORCE-MENTS!

HMPH! REALLY, ZICK...

I DON'T SEE ANY PLANT!

THAT'S BECAUSE IT'S SHY! IT'S HIDING, BUT IT CAN HEAR US!

JUST PRETEND IT'S RIGHT HERE IN FRONT OF YOU!

WHAT BRINGS YOU HERE AGAIN, LITTLE TAMER?

WE NEED TO GET TO THE CENTER OF BIGBURG, RIGHT UNDERNEATH THE BUILDING OF THE PYRAMID... AND I THOUGHT YOU MIGHT KNOW THE WAY.

YOU ALREADY KNOW THE ANSWER...

YOU HAVE THE GIFT OF COMMAND...

WE WILL DO AS YOU SAY...

...BECAUSE NO ONE CAN RESIST THE TONE OF THE TAMER!

THE TONE OF THE TAMER... I NEED TO REMEMBER TO ASK GRANDPA ABOUT IT...

WELL?

IT'S GOING TO HELP US! PASS ME THE FLASHLIGHT AND FOLLOW ME!

OH SURE, DON'T WORRY ABOUT ME...

WHAT ARE YOU TALKING ABOUT?

YOU NEVER TELL ME ANYTHING ABOUT THE MONSTERS YOU SEE! I TRUST YOU... I BELIEVE YOU... BUT SOONER OR LATER I'M GOING TO GET TIRED OF THIS!

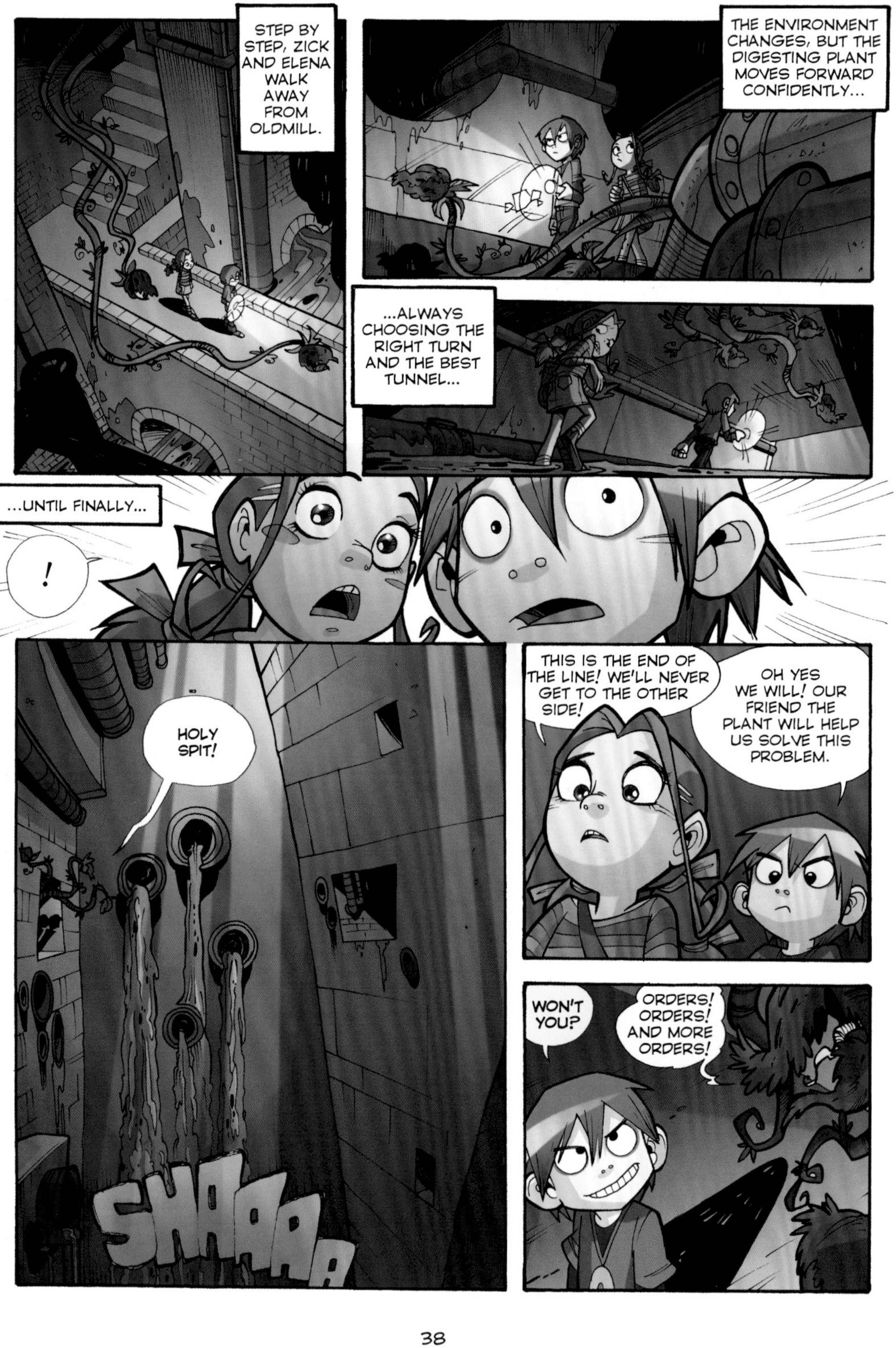
STEP BY STEP, ZICK AND ELENA WALK AWAY FROM OLDMILL.
THE ENVIRONMENT CHANGES, BUT THE DIGESTING PLANT MOVES FORWARD CONFIDENTLY...
...ALWAYS CHOOSING THE RIGHT TURN AND THE BEST TUNNEL...
...UNTIL FINALLY...
!
HOLY SPIT!
SHAAAAA
THIS IS THE END OF THE LINE! WE'LL NEVER GET TO THE OTHER SIDE!
OH YES WE WILL! OUR FRIEND THE PLANT WILL HELP US SOLVE THIS PROBLEM.
WON'T YOU?
ORDERS! ORDERS! AND MORE ORDERS!

SWIIIIP

SWIIISH

CRUNK

CRANCH

KTUNK

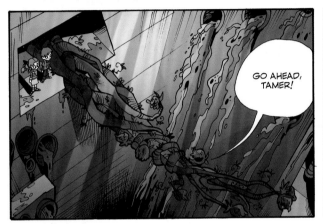

GO AHEAD, TAMER!

GIVE ME YOUR HAND, ELENA!

UH... HOLD ON! WHERE ARE YOU GOING?

THERE'S A BRIDGE HERE! THE DIGESTING PLANT MADE IT BY TWISTING TOGETHER ITS TENDRILS...

N-NO, ZICK! H-HANG ON! I...I...I CAN'T SEE ANYTHING!

YOU CAN'T SEE IT, BUT IT'S THERE! SHEESH, AREN'T YOU ALWAYS TELLING ME THAT YOU BELIEVE ME?

AHA! SO YOU LIKE THAT, DO YOU?

YEAH, YEAH, YEAH... BUT LET'S HURRY UP!

NOT SO FAST! I WANT TO HEAR YOU SAY IT PROPERLY!

ADMIT IT. YOU'RE HAPPY THAT SOMEONE FINALLY BELIEVES YOU.

GRRRR! I'LL MAKE YOU PAY FOR THIS!

SO, TO MAKE IT SHORT...I'M GLAD THAT I HAVE A FRIEND WHO TRUSTS ME.

THANKS, ZICK!

COME ON, MOVE IT!

I'LL EVEN FOLLOW YOU WITH MY EYES SHUT!

WE MADE IT! WE'RE A GREAT TEAM, YOU AND I!

FANTASTIC. LET ME TAKE A QUICK LOOK AT THIS MAP...

IT SAYS HERE THAT WE'RE AT THE LOWEST POINT OF THE BUILDING. SO ALL WE HAVE TO DO IS GO UP!

LET'S GO UP, THEN! NEW AND EXCITING MYSTERIES AWAIT US!

WHAT WILL WE FIND ABOVE US? WILL WE FIND OUR STOLEN CATS? BUT MOST IMPORTANT...

...WILL WE EVER BE ABLE TO GET RID OF THIS DISGUSTING SMELL?

WHAT DO YOU THINK, ZICK?

ZICK!

OH NO! ZICK!

I FELT IT, CLEAR AS DAY! HE'S... HE'S VERY CLOSE!

AND HE'S IN TERRIBLE DANGER!

YOU DON'T SAY! AND HERE I WAS THINKING I WAS IN TROUBLE!

RIGHT, YOU'RE THE LAST ONE! READY TO RUMBLE!

Meeeow!

HAVE A SAFE JOURNEY, KITTY CATS!

TELL ME, FOR GOODNESS SAKE! WHAT'S GOING ON?

IT'S TIMOTHY! HE'S UP THERE!

AT LEAST TELL ME WHERE YOU'RE GOING! ACCORDING TO THE MAP...

FORGET THE MAP! NOW TIMOTHY IS TELLING ME WHERE TO GO!

OF COURSE, MR. SFINKELMAYER! THE CONTRACT IS ABOUT TO BE SIGNED AND IN A COUPLE OF DAYS AND EVERYTHING WILL BE IN ORDER...

BUT NOW YOU MUST EXCUSE ME... I HAVE A CALL ON THE OTHER LINE.

FTLIP

HMMM...

NO...

PUAH!

NO!

TSK!

AHA! THIS TIME THEY'VE SAVED THE BEST FOR LAST!

HE'S RIGHT ABOVE US!

BUT THE TRAP DOOR IS CLOSED!

ON THE COUNT OF THREE, PULL AS HARD AS YOU CAN! ONE! TWO...

SNORT! WHAT A SMELL! THIS DANGED TOILET IS BLOCKED AG...

...AAAIII—IIIIIIIIIII—IINNN!

WHO WAS THAT?

WHO CARES! IF YOU REALLY WANT TO KNOW, WE'LL ASK HIM ON THE WAY BACK.

TUMP

WE'RE IN, ZICK...

IN THE BASEMENT, TO BE PRECISE...

WHERE THE CAT PRISON IS! I KNEW THEY KEPT THEM AROUND HERE SOMEWHERE!

SLAM

COME HERE, SWEETIES! YOU'RE FREE!

! ?

B-BUT...BUT WHY ARE THEY ACTING LIKE THAT?

BECAUSE WE'VE SPENT TWO HOURS KNEE-DEEP IN POOP, ELENA! IT'S A BIT MUCH FOR THEIR DELICATE NOSES...

PURRCY ISN'T HERE!

AND NEITHER IS TIMOTHY! HE'S MOVED AWAY AGAIN...

...AND HE WENT THIS WAY!

WHAT CAN YOU SEE, ZICK?

A TUTOR, VLADIMIR...

I REALLY FEEL THAT THERE IS A TUTOR HERE!

BUT WHICH IS THE RIGHT ONE, SUBLIME MAGNACAT?

WHICH WOULD YOU BET ON?

ON THE GIRL'S CAT, GREAT SIR! THE ONE BROUGHT TO YOU BY MY HUMBLE SELF!

YOU LOST! I CAN'T SEE THE SIGN WITH MY EYES! THERE IS NO TRACE OF THE TUTOR MARK ON THE ANIMAL!

A TUTOR MARK...

...LIKE THIS?

AHA!

HAVE YOU GONE CRAZY?

I KNOW WHAT I'M DOING... BUT MOST IMPORTANT I KNOW WHO YOU ARE, TIMOTHY!

AND I KNOW YOU'RE TOO IMPORTANT TO GO DOWN IN THIS BATTLE!

SO THIS IS YOUR TRUE FACE, MAGNA-CAT! BEHIND THE MASK THERE IS A GORKA!

...A DESPICABLE SHAPE-SHIFTER!

IT'S SAD HAVING TO PRETEND... ME RESEMBLING A HUMAN...

AND YOU DISGUISED AS A CAT...

WHATEVER IT IS YOU WANT, CREATURE...

...THE ANSWER IS NO!

SHA-WAAAAM

...BUT MY SKIN IS TOO THICK FOR HER!

RAAAARGH!

SIR!

GET BACK, VLADIMIR! THIS CAT STILL HAS SOME STING IN HER CLAWS...

AAAH!

SOON I WILL BE THE NEW LORD OF BIBBUR-SI AND YOU TUTORS WILL HELP ME CONQUER IT!

THE EXILED MONSTERS YOU WATCH OVER WILL BECOME MY ARMY! UNTIL NOW THE PEOPLE OF BIBBUR-SI HAVE FORBIDDEN THE GORKAS FROM LIVING WITH THEM...

...BUT STARTING TOMORROW, THE GORKAS WILL RULE THEIR ENTIRE CITY! HA HA HA!

TAKE HER AWAY, VLADIMIR! SHE WILL TELL ME EVERYTHING ABOUT THE TUTORS WHO ARE STILL OUT THERE...

...AND ABOUT THE PLACES WHERE THEIR HOMELESS MONSTERS ARE CONFINED...MY FUTURE ARMY! HA HA HA!

POW

URGH!

TIMO-THY!

PURRCY!

WHAT THE HECK HAVE YOU DONE TO MY CAT?

YOU AGAIN?!

THAT'S ENOUGH!

YOU'RE RIGHT, MAGNACAT...

SKRA-TRANG

...THAT IS ENOUGH!

KMINZ

STELLAR!

A STELLAR TUTOR! I CAN'T BELIEVE IT!

MY ANDROGORKAS WILL BE HAPPY TO GET SOME EXERCISE!

GET THEM!

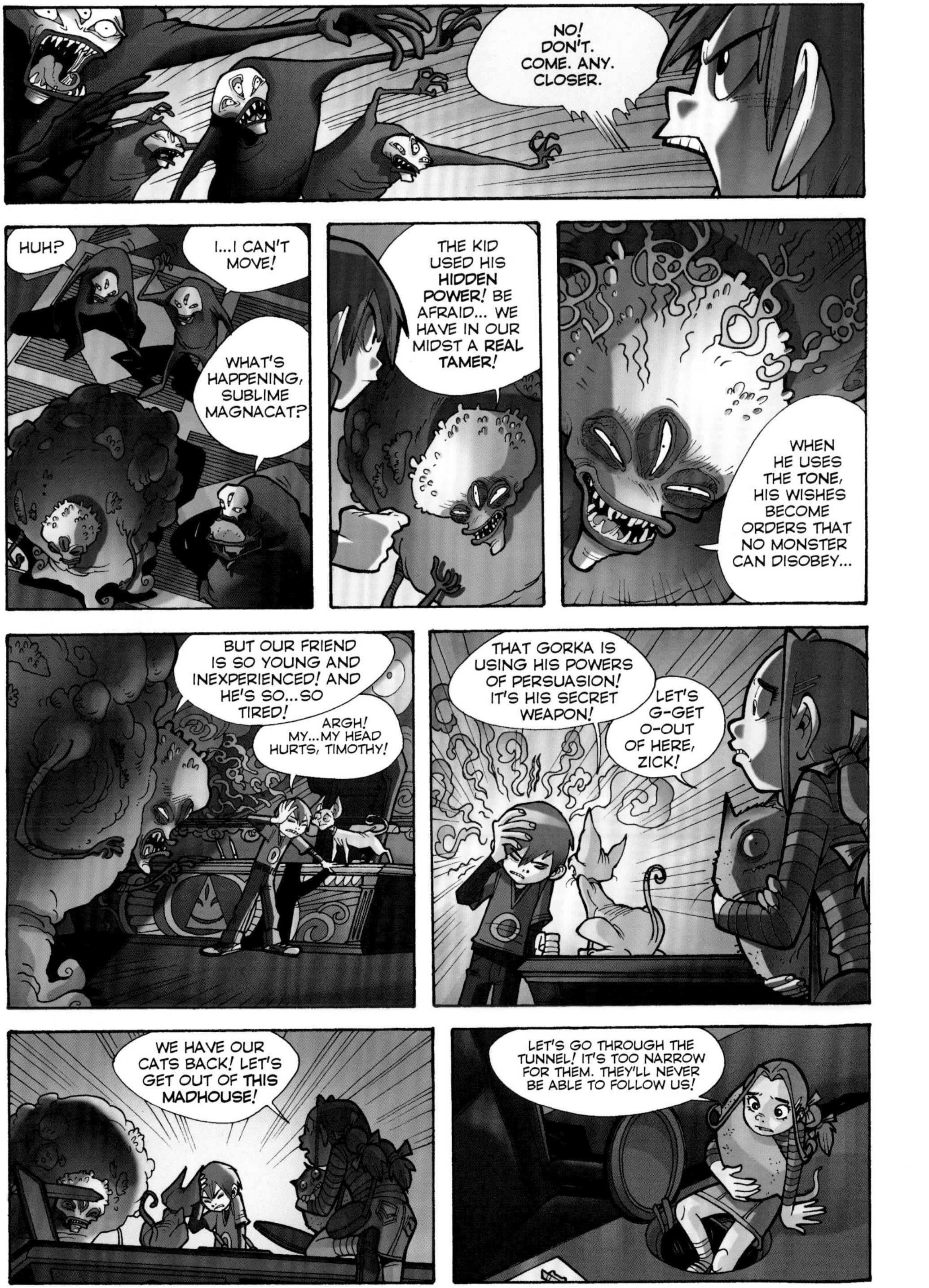
NO! DON'T. COME. ANY. CLOSER.
HUH?
I...I CAN'T MOVE!
WHAT'S HAPPENING, SUBLIME MAGNACAT?
THE KID USED HIS HIDDEN POWER! BE AFRAID... WE HAVE IN OUR MIDST A REAL TAMER!
WHEN HE USES THE TONE, HIS WISHES BECOME ORDERS THAT NO MONSTER CAN DISOBEY...
BUT OUR FRIEND IS SO YOUNG AND INEXPERIENCED! AND HE'S SO...SO TIRED!
ARGH! MY...MY HEAD HURTS, TIMOTHY!
THAT GORKA IS USING HIS POWERS OF PERSUASION! IT'S HIS SECRET WEAPON!
LET'S G-GET O-OUT OF HERE, ZICK!
WE HAVE OUR CATS BACK! LET'S GET OUT OF THIS MADHOUSE!
LET'S GO THROUGH THE TUNNEL! IT'S TOO NARROW FOR THEM. THEY'LL NEVER BE ABLE TO FOLLOW US!

OKAY! I CAN'T TAKE ANY- MORE...

BUT WE CAN'T LEAVE HER!

GO, TIMOTHY!

DON'T WORRY! WE'LL COME BACK FOR YOU...

LARDINE... MY NAME IS LARDINE!

WE'LL MEET AGAIN!

BE SURE OF IT!

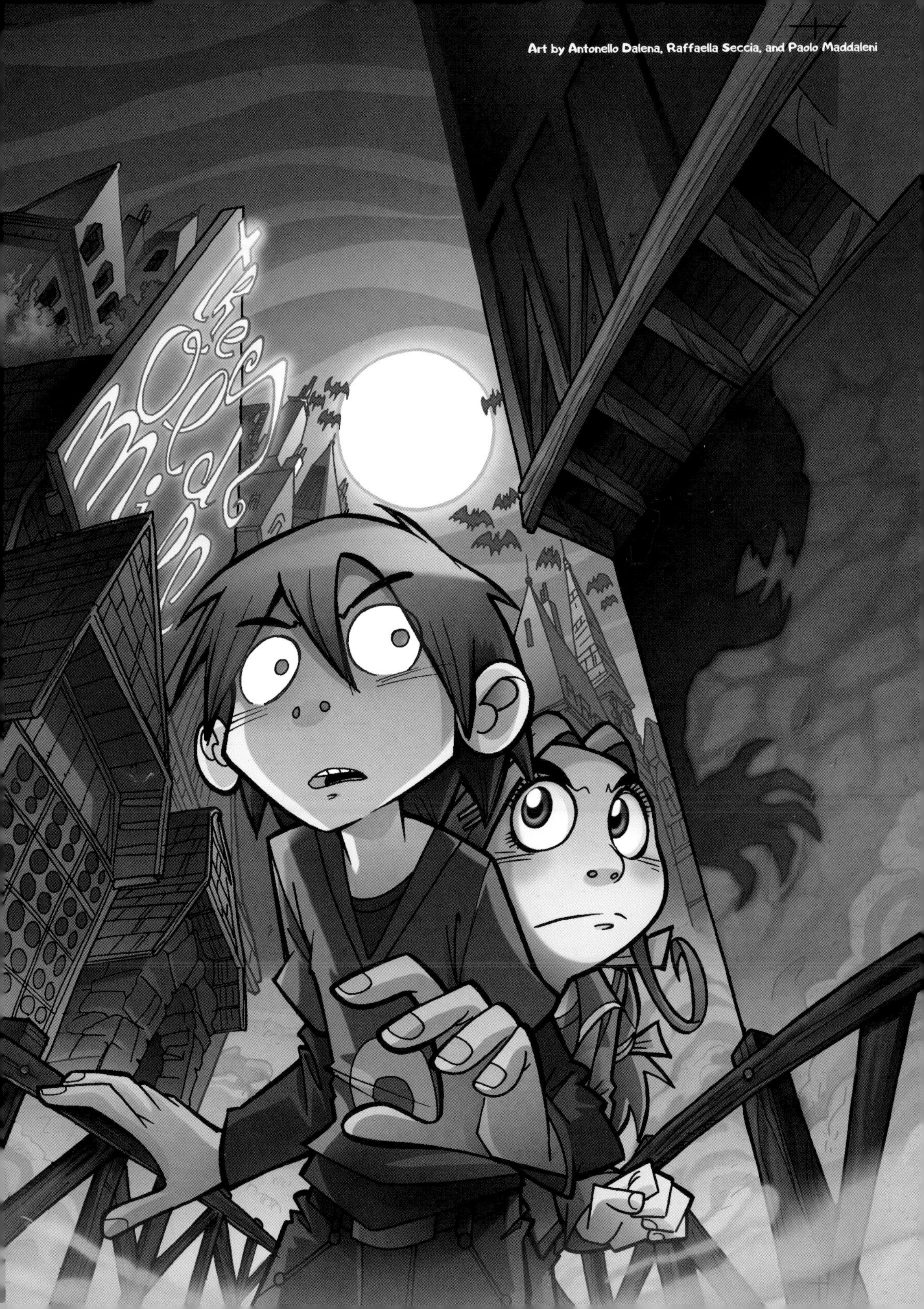
the Old Mill
Art by Antonello Dalena, Raffaella Seccia, and Paolo Maddaleni

PART 2

THE SUSPENDED CITY

Plot: Katja Centomo
Script: Francesco Artibani
Pencils: Paolo Campinoti
Inks: Santa Zangari
Design Supervisor: Alessandro Barbucci
Colors: Pamela Brughera,
Sergio Algozzino,
and Barbara Bargiggia
Colors Supervisor: Barbara Canepa

Art by Paolo Campinoti, Cristina Giorgilli, and Barbara Bargiggia

SCHOOL STARTS IN A FEW DAYS.

SUMMER VACATION IS COMING TO AN END.

RIGHT NOW, ZICK AND ELENA WOULD LOVE TO BE IN THE CLASSROOM, AT THEIR DESKS SURROUNDED BY BOOKS.

THIS ISN'T TOO SUR-PRISING...

...SEEING AS THEY'RE FALLING DOWN A BOTTOM-LESS HOLE.

ABOVE THEM IS MR. MAGNACAT.

BELOW THEM ONLY DARKNESS.

NO WONDER THEY CAN'T WAIT TO GET BACK TO POP QUIZZES AND SPELLING TESTS.

MEEEEOOOW!

AHHHHHHH!

EEEEEK!

SWIKS"

YIKES!

AHHHHHH!

SHAAAA

HUH?

BUMP

SPLAT

TUNG

BOING

TOC

I...I CAN'T BELIEVE IT! WE'RE SAVED!

PLANT! YOU WAITED FOR US?

WHERE DO YOU THINK WE'D HAVE GONE?

YOU'RE OUR MASTER NOW.

I'VE GOT A GREEN THUMB!

YOU SOUND LIKE MY MOM! HA! HA! HA!

THANK YOUR INVISIBLE PLANT FOR ME!

DID YOU HEAR THAT? NOW TAKE US HOME...

"IT'S BEEN A LONG DAY."

TOMORROW WE'LL TALK AND I'LL EXPLAIN THINGS TO HER.

YOU DON'T OWE ANYONE ANY EXPLANATIONS. CERTAIN THINGS SHOULD BE KEPT SECRET.

YOU'VE MADE PROGRESS...AND I DON'T LIKE IT!

KFFFF

I'M AWAY FOR TWO SECONDS AND YOU DECIDE TO PLAY AROUND WITH THE TONE OF THE TAMER!

THERE WAS A LOT GOING ON! I THINK YOU NEED TO EXPLAIN EVERYTHING FROM THE BEGINNING.

FOR EXAMPLE, WHO WAS THAT CAT IN MAGNA-CAT'S OFFICE?

HER NAME IS LARDINE...

...AND SHE SACRIFICIED HERSELF FOR ME! SHE PROTECTED ME FROM BEING CAPTURED.

DON'T TELL ME THAT THING SHINING ON YOUR CHEST IS A HEART!

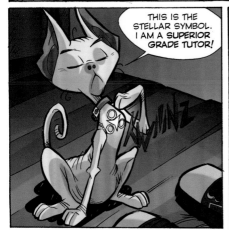

THIS IS THE STELLAR SYMBOL. I AM A SUPERIOR GRADE TUTOR!

KWINZ

AND MAGNACAT? WHO'S HE?

A MONSTER OF THE WORST KIND! HE'S A SHAPE-CHANGING CREATURE...A GORKA!

53

THE MONSTER WORLD IS GREAT BECAUSE IT'S SO VARIED! THERE ARE BOMBOS, BOBAKS, SNYA-KUTS, BURSTS, GINGIS...

...AND THEN, THERE ARE THE GORKA.

GORKA ARE AN EVIL RACE WHO CAN CHANGE THE WAY THEY LOOK... AND CONTROL YOUR MIND!

THAT'S WHY THEY HAVE ALWAYS BEEN KEPT AWAY FROM MONSTER CITIES...

AND NOW HE WANTS REVEN-GE!

TO BE PRECISE, HE WANTS TO HUMILIATE BIBBUR-SI BECAUSE IT REJECTED HIM... AND HE'S BUILDING AN ARMY TO ATTACK THE CITY!

AN AWMY?! I AM SOMEVAT VORRIED!

HIS ARMY WILL CONSIST OF ANDRO-GORKAS...

...PEOPLE WHO HAVE TRADED THEIR HUMANITY FOR MAGNACAT'S POTION OF LONG LIFE!

THE MEMBERS OF THE PYRAMID OF THE INVUL-NERABLE!

NOT JUST THEM! MAGNACAT WANTS TO RECRUIT THE FORCES OF EXILED MONSTERS...

 ...DESPERATE CREATURES CONDEMNED AND CAST OUT BY THEIR HOMETOWNS...

 ...SCORNED BY THEIR FAMILIES, DISOWNED BY THEIR RACE...

 ...CREATURES LIKE YOU!

!

 ME THINK ME IS NICE!

OH, BUT YOU ARE NICE!

A VERY NICE THIEF!

 NOW I UNDERSTAND WHAT GRANDPA WAS TRYING TO TELL ME!*

WELL, I MIGHT HAVE DRAMATIZED IT A BIT...

*SEE PART 1

 ...LET'S SAY THEY'RE IMMATURE MONSTERS ON MANDATORY VACATION TO PROTECT THEM FROM THEMSELVES!

 IN THIS GHOST NEIGHBORHOOD THE MONSTERS DON'T DARE TO GO OUT! THAT IS OUR IDEA OF EXILE!

 YOU ARE MONSTERS IN EXILE...

 ...AND I AM YOUR TUTOR!

IT EEZ NOT APLOPLIATE TO DRAW TOO MUCH ATTENTION TO ZEES BUSINESS!

FINALLY WE'RE GETTING SOME EXPLANATIONS. YOU SHOULD TAKE NOTES, BOY!

MORE SECRETS! THAT'S IT, I'VE HAD ENOUGH!

I'M NOT INTERESTED IN WHAT THEY'VE DONE! ALL I WANT TO KNOW IS WHY YOU'RE TELLING ME ALL THIS!

BECAUSE NOW YOU ARE PART OF SOMETHING BIGGER...

...JUST LIKE THEY'RE PART OF SOMETHING THAT GOES BEYOND THE WALLS OF THIS HOUSE!

I TELL YOU SO THAT YOU UNDERSTAND! IF SOMETHING SHOULD HAP-PEN TO ME, YOU SHOULD KNOW HOW TO LOOK AFTER YOURSELVES!

IS THAT A POSSIBILITY?

MAGNACAT IS LOOKING FOR TUTORS LIKE ME TO REACH EXILED MONSTERS LIKE YOU!

THAT'S WHY HE'S ORGANIZED THIS BIG CAT HUNT!

WITHOUT TUTORS TO LOOK AFTER THEM, HE'LL TAKE OVER THE MINDS OF THESE FRAGILE MONSTERS.

AND THERE ARE MORE THAN YOU COULD IMAGINE!

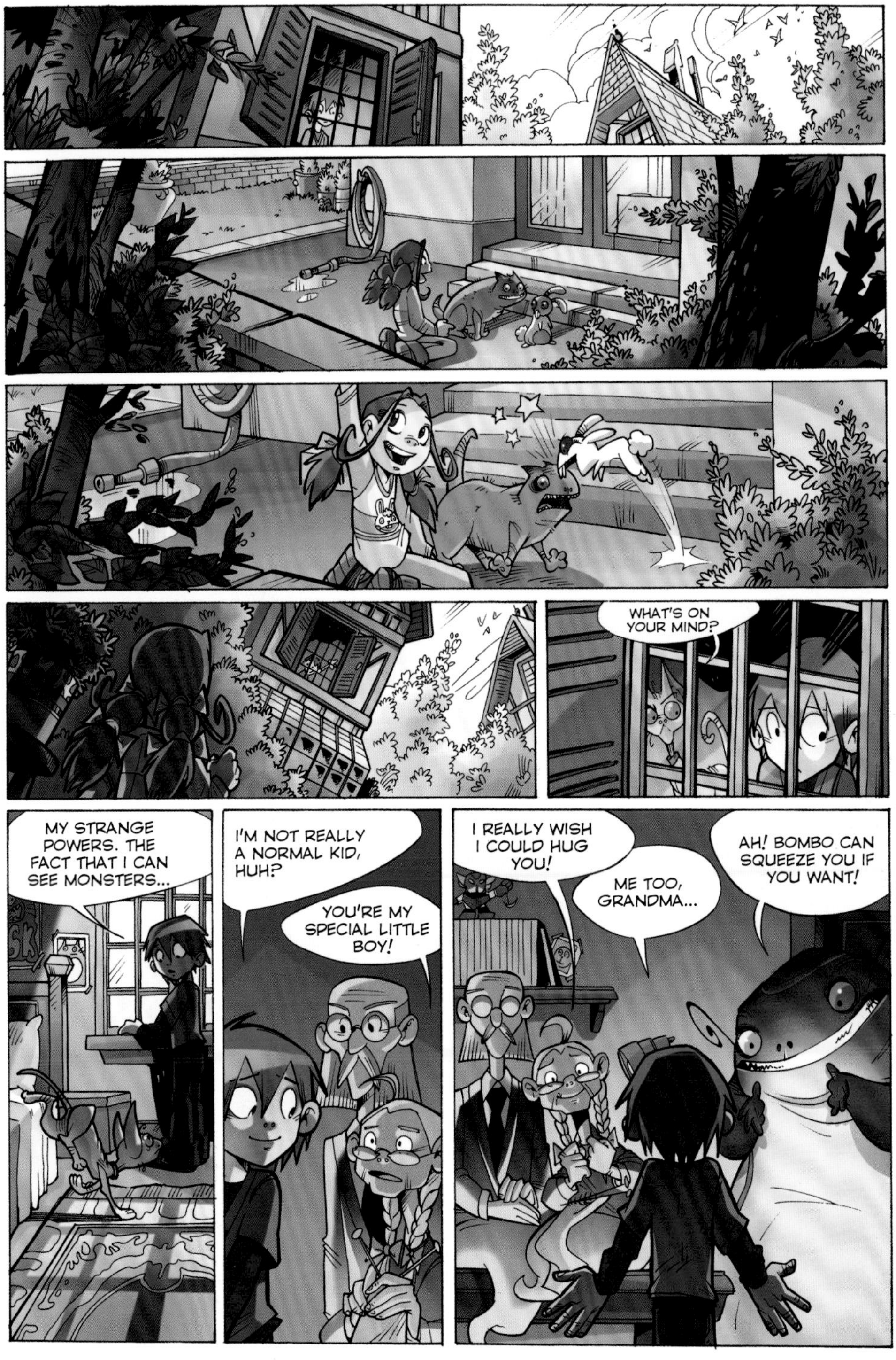

WHAT'S ON YOUR MIND?
MY STRANGE POWERS. THE FACT THAT I CAN SEE MONSTERS...
I'M NOT REALLY A NORMAL KID, HUH?
YOU'RE MY SPECIAL LITTLE BOY!
I REALLY WISH I COULD HUG YOU!
ME TOO, GRANDMA...
AH! BOMBO CAN SQUEEZE YOU IF YOU WANT!

WHAT A MOVING LITTLE INTERLUDE. CAN WE TALK ABOUT IMPORTANT THINGS NOW?

WE ARE AT WAR WITH MAGNACAT, LADIES AND GENTLEMEN! HE KNOWS WHO WE ARE AND WE KNOW HIS SECRET!

I SAY WE HAVE TO MAKE THE NEXT MOVE!

WHAT, USING THE TONE...

ONLY BECAUSE WE HAVE NO ALTERNATIVE!

OK... IF I CAN MAKE MONSTERS OBEY ME, THEN I CAN ALSO DEAL WITH MAGNACAT!

I WANT TO STOP THE PYRAMID OF THE INVULNERABLE...AND SAVE LARDINE AND ALL THE CATS STILL IMPRISONED.

HMMM...

TAKE IT EASY... AND REMEMBER, LEAVE THE GIRL OUT OF IT!

B-BUT... WHY?

ELENA IS COOL!

I HAVE ALREADY LET YOU GET AWAY WITH TOO MUCH AND ELENA KNOWS TOO MUCH! THIS TIME, WE HAVE TO MOVE ON OUR OWN!

"WE'LL STRIKE TONIGHT, ZICK! WE'RE GOING TO BIBBUR-SI..."

"...AND WE'LL ENTER THROUGH THE MAIN GATE!"

WAS IT REALLY NECESSARY TO DRESS ME UP LIKE THIS?

YES, WAN... THR... UNNC...

⸨GASP!⸩ IS IT FAR?

HANG IN THERE! WE'RE NEARLY THERE!

OH, I NEARLY FORGOT...

SFLOP

⸨PFFFFFT⸩ ⸨PFFFFFT⸩ ⸨PFFFFFT⸩

NOW YOU'RE A PERFECT GINGI!

I FEEL RIDICU-LOUS!

GINGI ARE RIDICULOUS! JUST ACT NATURALLY, ZICK...

...AND WHATEVER YOU DO, DON'T EVER SAY YOU'RE A TAMER!

WHY NOT?

MONSTERS ARE INDEPENDENT CREATURES! THEY DON'T LIKE HAVING SOMEONE GIVING ORDERS WHO ALSO THINKS HE'S THE BOSS!

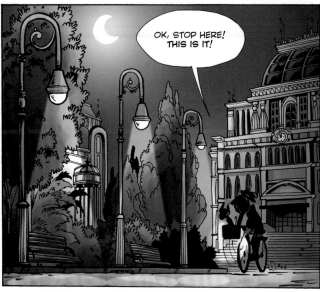

OK, STOP HERE! THIS IS IT!

THAT'S THE ENTRANCE TO BIBBUR-SI, ZICK! I'M SO EXCITED...

THAT?

...SO MUCH TIME HAS GONE BY, BUT **THE KIOSK** IS STILL IN ITS PLACE!

Ronnie Ricino
FRUITCAKE

FRUITCAKE? WHAT'S THAT SUPPOSED TO BE?

DELICACIES THAT HUMANS NO LONGER APPRECIATE! I'D PAY A MILLION DOLLARS TO TASTE A CRUMB...

...OR YOU COULD TREAT ME! HOW MUCH MONEY DO YOU HAVE?

I'M NOT GOING UP TO HIM LOOKING LIKE THIS!

OH, RICINO IS USED TO SEEING WEIRD THINGS! HURRY UP, WILL YOU?

TIMOTHY!

PLEASE, JUST DON'T ASK.

I JUST SELL CAKES. EVERYTHING ELSE IS NONE OF MY BUSINESS.

OVER HERE, ZICK!

I HAVE NEVER BEEN SO EMBARASSED IN MY LIFE!

CAN WE TALK ABOUT IT LATER?

THE MIDNIGHT ELEVATOR IS ARRIVING!

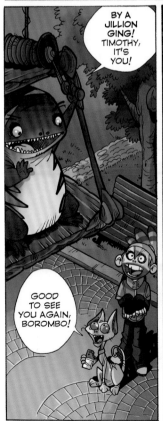

BY A JILLION GING! TIMOTHY, IT'S YOU!

GOOD TO SEE YOU AGAIN, BOROMBO!

OHH...

AND IT'S GOOD TO SEE BIBBUR-SI AGAIN, TOO!

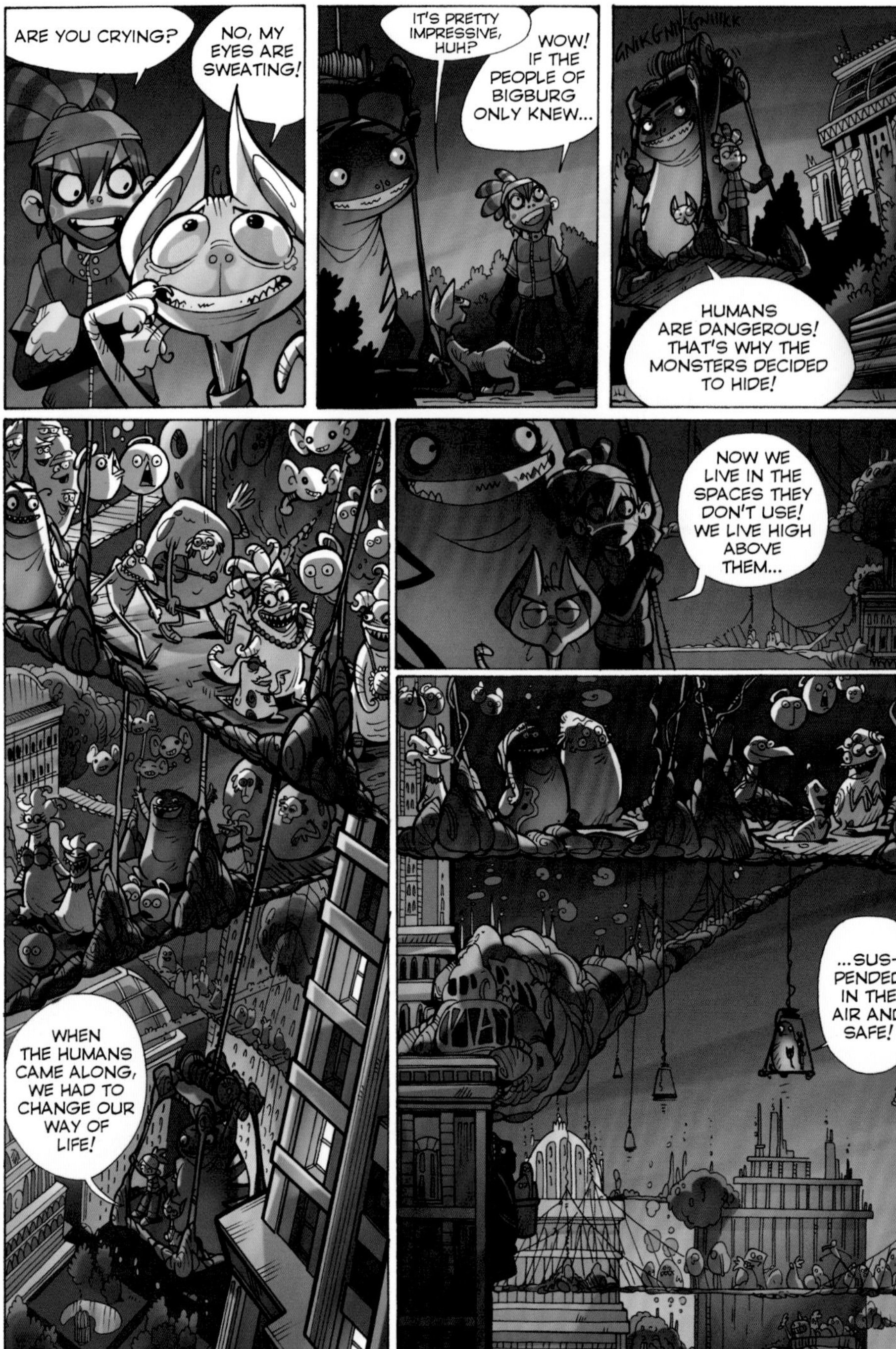
ARE YOU CRYING?
NO, MY EYES ARE SWEATING!
IT'S PRETTY IMPRESSIVE, HUH?
WOW! IF THE PEOPLE OF BIGBURG ONLY KNEW...
GNIKGNIKGNIIKK
HUMANS ARE DANGEROUS! THAT'S WHY THE MONSTERS DECIDED TO HIDE!
WHEN THE HUMANS CAME ALONG, WE HAD TO CHANGE OUR WAY OF LIFE!
NOW WE LIVE IN THE SPACES THEY DON'T USE! WE LIVE HIGH ABOVE THEM...
...SUS-PENDED IN THE AIR AND SAFE!

CLUNK

LAST STOP, GENTLEMEN!

PUFF PUFF

WE'RE HERE...

SEE YOU AROUND, TIMOTHY! DON'T WAIT ANOTHER FOUR HUNDRED YEARS TO STOP BY AGAIN!

WOW! YOU'RE THAT OLD?

IF YOU DON'T MIND THE TERM IS "MATURE." BESIDES, FOR US MONSTERS, AGE IS A RELATIVE CONCEPT!

HAAAA... THAT'S WHAT AUNT EMILY SAYS, TOO...

ATCHOO!

HEY! CONSIDERING YOU A GINGI YOU'RE LOST PIECES LIKE A SNYAKUZ!

ARE YOU SURE YOU'RE OK?

IT'S ONLY MY USUAL ALLERGY...

LET ME THROUGH! I'M A DOCTOR!

IF YOU LIKE, I'LL CAST AN EYE OVER YOU! HA! HA! HA!

POP

AN EYE! HA! HA! HA!

OH, I GET IT, AN EYE! HA! HA! HA!

IDIOTS!

LET'S GET OUT OF HERE. KEEP CLOSE, ZICK!

YOU'VE THOUGHT OF EVERYTHING, EXCEPT FOR THE PEOPLE OF BIGBURG!

WHAT DO YOU MEAN?

IF SOMEONE DOWN THERE LOOKS UP, THEY WON'T SEE THE CITY OF MONSTERS...

...BUT THEY WILL SEE A BOY SUSPENDED IN MIDAIR, BETWEEN THE BUILDINGS! I'M NOT INVISIBLE, TIMOTHY!

RELAX! NO ONE PAYS ANY ATTENTION TO EACH OTHER IN BIGBURG...

...IT'S A HECTIC WORLD, ZICK!

AND THERE'S NEVER ANYONE AROUND AT NIGHT. NOW GET IN...

...AND ENJOY THE RIDE! IF YOU'VE NEVER TAKEN A TRANSPORTATION MONSTER BEFORE IT'LL BE AN UNFORGETTABLE JOURNEY!

ERM... COULD YOU SQUEEZE IN A BIT, PLEASE?

WE'RE SO LUCKY THAT WE MADE IT! THIS IS THE LAST RIDE FOR TONIGHT!

"AND THERE'S SO MUCH TRAFFIC AT THIS TIME OF NIGHT!"

64

REALLY AN UNFORGETTABLE JOURNEY! THANKS, TIMOTHY!

GASP! IN MY DAY TRAVELING WAS A LOT MORE COMFORTABLE!

THERE'S STILL ONE THING YOU HAVEN'T EXPLAINED TO ME...

WHAT'S THAT?

WHERE ARE WE GOING?

TO SEE SOMEONE WHO CAN HELP US!

HE HAS ENCOUNTERED MANY CREATURES LIKE MAGNACAT IN THE COURSE OF HIS CAREER!

HE'S MERCILESS! LETHAL! RELENTLESS!

HE'S A LIVING LEGEND, ZICK! HE'S THE GREATEST GORKA HUNTER EVER...

"HIS NAME IS TRENGINGIGAN!"

KRRRR-ZZZZ! ZZZZ-KRRRR!

KRRRRR-ZZZZ! ZZZZ-KRRRRR!

RELENTLESS, HUH?

NOT ANOTHER WORD!

KRRRR-ZZZZ! ZZZZ-KRRRRR!

KRRRRR-ZZZZ! ZZZZ-KRRRRRR!

MASTER? ERM... MASTER?

KRRRRR-ZZZZ! ZZZZ-KRRRRRRRR!

BUT... HUH?

FLIP

AAAAIIIIIYAAAA!

AAA-AAAHHH

!

YIKES!

KRASH KA-TRANG

MASTER!

TIMOTHY! FIREFLIES AND MOTHS! IT'S REALLY YOU!

AND WHO ARE YOU? I'VE NEVER SEEN YOU BEFORE! AT LEAST NOT WITH MY GOOD EYE!

HE'S...HE'S A FRIEND OF MINE, MASTER TRENGING! GAN! JUST A GING! WHO'S PASSING THROUGH!

YOU'RE STILL ON THE BALL, EH? NOTHING CAN SURPRISE YOU!

I'VE BEEN A FIGHTER ALL MY LIFE... I'VE LEARNED TO SLEEP WITH ONE EYE OPEN!

HA! HA! HA!

THAT WASN'T A JOKE.

OOPS.

SO, WHAT BRINGS YOU TO THESE PARTS?

KATAKRUM

BONK

I'VE BROKEN MORE THAN ONE RULE TO BE HERE, BUT I HAVE A VERY GOOD REASON...

A GORKA NAMED MAGNACAT!

HMM... MAGNACAT! NEVER HEARD OF HIM...

YOU'D LIKE HIM! HE'S A TOUGH ONE.

HORRID CREATURES. I'VE SEEN SO MANY OF THEM IN MY LIFE...

TOO MANY.

THIS WOUND I PICKED UP ON RAVEN ISLAND...

THE PLATE IN MY HEAD IS A SOUVENIR FROM A BATTLE ON ARMO-TAU...

TOC TOC TOC TOC

AND THAT?

MY WIFE! SHE MADE ME PAY AN EYE FOR AN EYE IN OUR DIVORCE SETTLEMENT!

FIZZY FOAM ALL ROUND?

I HAVEN'T GOT ANY SECRET TIPS OR TRICKS TO HELP YOU FIGHT A GORKA, BUT I CAN GIVE YOU **THIS!**

A MIRROR?

YOU NEED IT TO CONFRONT THOSE BEINGS WITHOUT LOOKING INTO THEIR EYES! THEIR POWERS OF PERSUASION ARE IRRESISTIBLE!

GO AHEAD AND KEEP IT! IT'S YOURS!

TLUNK

REALLY? HOW CAN WE EVER THANK YOU, MASTER?

BRING ME MAGNACAT'S HEAD! IT'LL REMIND ME OF TIMES GONE BY...

SUP SUP SUP

...WHEN THE ONLY GOOD GORKA WAS AN **IMPALED** GORKA!

ERM... SEE YOU SOON, MASTER! WE'LL KEEP YOU POSTED!

YES, TIMOTHY...

...SEE YOU SOON.

ARE YOU SURE YOU'RE OK, ZICK?

YOU STAYED UP LATE READING LAST NIGHT, DIDN'T YOU?

ZZZZZ

OPEN YOUR EYES! THIS WAS IN THE LETTERBOX FOR YOU.

TO ZICK

HUH?

I'M OFF! LUNCH IS IN THE MICROWAVE. BE GOOD AND ALL THAT, OKAY?

OKAY, MOM!

SNIFF! SNORT... SNIFF...

ATCHOOO!

WELL, WELL, WELL... IS IT A SCENTED LETTER, SON?

YEAH... AND I DON'T LIKE WHAT I SMELL! IT'S A LETTER THAT SMELLS LIKE MONSTER!

NO, ZICK...

...IT'S A LETTER THAT SMELLS OF MAG-NACAT!

RRRRIIIIIP!

TO ZICK

AND IT'S SIGNED BY HIM PERSONALLY!

WHAT DOES IT SAY?

I NEED TO DICTATE A LETTER...

WHO SHALL I ADDRESS IT TO?

TO MY NEW FRIENDS! A LITTLE BOY AND HIS CAT...

THEY HAVE SOMETHING I WANT... AND THEY WANT SOMETHING FROM ME...

I'LL GIVE THEM LARDINE...

...IN EXCHANGE FOR A FRIENDLY DISCUSSION ABOUT A VERY ADVANTAGEOUS OFFER!

HE'LL BE WAITING FOR US IN ONE HOUR ON THE BEACH OF GLOOMY BAY! HE MUST BE FEELING VERY SURE OF HIMSELF TO LEAVE HIS HOME TURF!

WILL YOU GO?

I WON'T ABANDON LARDINE! IF THAT GORKA ATTACKS, WE WILL DEFEND OURSELVES!

RIGHT! WE HAVE THE MIRROR!

YES...BUT WE HAVE TO BE VERY CAREFUL.

DON'T WORRY, TIMMY! IF YOU DIES, WE MANAGE ON OUR OWN!

SO TELL ME...IF YOU SNUFF IT, CAN I HAVE YOUR BOOKS?

HMPH! YOUR AFFECTION MOVES ME!

SWINES! SCUM THEY ARE AND SCUM THEY ALWAYS WILL BE UNTIL THE END OF THEIR USELESS DAYS!

THIS JOB GETS ME NOTHING BUT TROUBLE!

BUT YOU'RE A STELLAR TUTOR! WITH GREAT POWER COMES GREAT RESPONSIBILITY!

DO! NOT! SAY! THAT! POWER ONLY EVER COMES WITH A PAIN IN THE BUTT!

MY PURPOSE AS A STELLAR TUTOR IS TO KEEP THESE SCOUNDRELS IN LINE, NOT THE OTHER WAY AROUND!

STILL, WE'RE A GREAT TEAM, YOU AND I! MASTER AND PUPIL!

RUBBISH! I'M NOT TEACHING YOU ANYTHING! I'VE JUST EXPLAINED THINGS YOU DON'T UNDERSTAND!

THIS BUSINESS WITH MAGNACAT IS AN EXCEPTIONAL EMERGENCY...

...AND IT WILL BE THE ONE AND ONLY TIME WE WILL EVER TAKE SUCH A RISK!

"IF ANYONE KNEW WHAT I GOT UP TO IN BIBBUR-SI, I WOULD BE DEMOTED IMMEDIATELY!"

I DON'T LIKE THIS PLACE! IT MAKES ME FEEL WEIRD...

IT'S MAGNACAT'S PRESENCE! HE'S COMING.

IS THE MIRROR IN PLACE?

UH HUH...

IF YOU'RE NOT UP TO IT, YOU CAN ALWAYS GO HOME!

I'M FINE, TIMOTHY!

LET'S GET READY! YOU KNOW THE PLAN! YOU KNOW WHAT YOU HAVE TO DO...

GOOD LUCK, TAMER!

GOOD LUCK TO YOU TOO, TUTOR!

I STILL FEEL A PRESENCE... IT'S STRONG... AND ALL AROUND ME...

WOOOSHH

?

CRUMB CRUNK

HI, ZICK.

!

HMM...

ANYBODY HOME?

AHAH! ME GOT HIM, GUYS! ME GOT HIM!

SWAK!

ZTOP RIGHT ZERE, INTWUDER! VAN MOVE AND YOU'RE MINCEMEAT!

WHO ARE YOU? WHAT DO YOU WANT? WHAT ARE YOU DOING HERE?

OHH...

WE DEFEND US WELL, RIGHT? TIMOTHY BE PROUD OF ME!

I DON'T THINK SO...YOU'VE JUST CLOBBERED A NATIONAL HERO!

HE'S THE GREAT TRENGINGIGAN! I'VE SEEN HIS PHOTO IN THE MONSTER GAZETTE!

ME TOO! BUT HE DEEED NOT 'HAVE ZAT BUMP.

SIIIIIILENCE!

I AM HERE TO WARN TIMOTHY AND HIS FRIEND!

WHAT?

EHM?

THEY'RE WALKING INTO A TRAP! THE BOMBO IN MY PANTRY SAW EVERYTHING!

WHAT ARE YOU TALKING ABOUT?

TIMOTHY COULDN'T HAVE KNOWN! THE MONSTER HE MET IN MY HOUSE WASN'T ME! BUT A DESPICABLE SHAPE-CHANGE GORKA!

I REALLY DON'T KNOW WHY ONE OF THOSE CREATURES DARED TO DO A THING LIKE THAT!

THIS IS MAGNACAT'S DOING!

I'M OUT OF TOWN FOR A COUPLE OF DAYS AND LOOK WHAT HAPPENS!

TIMOTHY AND ZICK NEED TO BE WARNED!

BUT WE CAN'T LEAVE THE DETENTION OASIS.

WELL THEN WE'LL HAVE TO SEND ELENA!

BUT ZEE GIRL, SHE CANNOT SEE US!

OK, SO WE'LL USE SOMEONE ELSE TO TALK TO HER!

"...LIKE HER STRANGE RABBIT!"

THERE IT IS! DON'T LET HIM GET AWAY, BOMBO!

YOU BE CALM! ME KNOW WHAT ME DOING!

HI THERE, LITTLE GUY!

?

YAAAAARGH!

SIGH!

GRRRRRRR OOAAAR!

74

HANG ON, PURRCY! AT LEAST TAKE A LOOK BEFORE YOU SAY NO!

WELL?

MEOW.

TRY THIS ONE, AND KEEP AN OPEN MIND! IT'LL TAKE SOME TIME BEFORE YOUR FUR GROWS BACK!

YOU DON'T WANT TO PARADE AROUND NAKED, DO YOU?

MMM...

WHAT DO YOU THINK, FLUFFY?

BUNNY-GRAM FOR ELENA!

EEEEEEK!

I HAVE A MESSAGE FROM THE WORLD OF MONSTERS! I'M ONLY SAYING IT ONCE...

...SO LISTEN CAREFULLY!

THERE'S NO NEED TO BE AFRAID OF ME, ZICK! THINGS ARE NEVER HOW THEY SEEM...

I CAN TELL THAT YOU HAVE THE TRUE CHARACTER OF A MONSTER TAMER...

THE TWO OF US COULD DO GREAT THINGS TOGETHER...

...IF YOU DESIRE IT!

AN ALLIANCE?! IS THAT YOUR PROPOSAL?

I'VE HAD A VISION! A DREAM OF GREATNESS...

WITH YOUR POWER AND THE ENERGY OF A STELLAR TUTOR, IT COULD BECOME REALITY!

NO, DON'T COME ANY CLOSER!

I'VE ALREADY TOLD YOU, ZICK! YOU DON'T NEED TO BE AFRAID OF ME!

WHERE IS LARDINE?

OH, LARDINE...

WHY DON'T YOU TELL ME WHERE YOUR KITTY CAT IS?

SHOULDN'T HE BE HERE TOO?

THAT SCOUNDREL IS TRYING TO USE HIS POWERS OF PERSUASION! BE STRONG, ZICK, BE STRONG!

YOU JUST HAVE TO FIND OUT WHERE HE'S KEEPING LARDINE AND...

AHA! I KNEW YOU WOULDN'T BE FAR!

MASTER! WHAT ARE YOU DOING HERE?

I WAS LOOKING FOR YOU, MY FRIEND! MAGNACAT WAS SURE THAT YOU'D BE HIDDEN SOMEWHERE NEARBY...

...BECAUSE A TUTOR NEVER TURNS DOWN A CHALLENGE...

?

HONOR AND RESPECT! THEY ARE PRECIOUS QUALITIES...

PLOC PLIC BLOORCH

...BUT WE GORKAS FIND THEM INCREDIBLY BORING!

YOU AREN'T TRENGINGIGAN!

MY NAME IS OMNISED! NUMBER ONE SERVANT OF THE SUBLIME MAGNACAT! MASTER OF DISGUISE! CHAMPION OF SUBTERFUGE!

HOW DO YOU FIT ALL THAT ON YOUR BUSINESS CARD?

YOUR JOKES HAVE NO PLACE HERE, TUTOR!

ZICK! BE CAREFUL!

NO, NO, NO, TIMOTHY... NO HELP IS ALLOWED!

SHA-WHAM

AH... SO THAT'S WHERE YOUR CAT WAS! WERE YOU TRYING TO SURPRISE ME? OR DID YOU WANT TO KEEP AN EYE ON ME?

WHAT DO YOU THINK?

I'M NOT HERE TO FIGHT, ZICK... I'M HERE TO TALK ABOUT MY PLAN! A DREAM OF ORDER AND CLEANSING!

WE CAN CONQUER THE WORLD WITH THOSE IDEAS!

ENOUGH! GET BACK!

YOUR POWERS OF COMMAND ARE IMPRESSIVE! JOIN FORCES WITH ME, ZICK...

HE'S RESISTING ME, DANG IT...

...AND YOU'LL GROW EVEN STRONGER!

THE MIRROR! I NEED TO LOOK AT HIM IN THE MIRROR!

IT'S A TRAP!

THE EASIEST TRICK OF MY CAREER!

I FOLLOWED ZICK AFTER HIS FIRST VISIT TO MY MASTER, AND I KEPT AN EYE ON HIM...

FTUNK

I KNEW YOU'D GO RUNNING TO THAT IDIOT TRENGIN-GIGAN!

SO I TOOK HIS PLACE...AND YOU FELL FOR IT! HA! HA! HA!

SO, ZICK?

ANYONE WHO LOOKS AT A GORKA IN A MIRROR IS A GONNER!

DUMP

B'DUMP

I'M WAITING FOR AN ANSWER!

MAGNACAT'S POWERS OF PERSUASION WILL BE STRENGTHENED A HUNDRED-FOLD... HE'LL GET INTO THE BOY'S HEAD...

SHUNK

YARGH!

...AND HIS BRAIN WILL TURN TO MUSH!

DON'T DO IT, ZICK! THROW AWAY THAT MIRROR!

HUH?

!

HUH?

HUH?

DON'T LOOK AT ME LIKE THAT! I DIDN'T SAY A WORD!

ELENA? WHAT ARE YOU DOING HERE?

I'M HERE TO SAVE YOUR SKIN! THE MIRROR IS A CON! DON'T USE IT AGAINST MAGNACAT!

!

GET HER, SANSON!

HOLD IT, KID!

GRMP!

AN INTERESTING DEVELOPMENT I'D SAY! WATCH YOUR NEXT STEP, ZICK...

...BECAUSE IF YOU TRY TO USE YOUR POWERS, YOUR LITTLE FRIEND WILL SUFFER!

THE LESSON IS OVER NOW!

I THINK YOU'RE WRONG OMNISED...

AAAAAMM

...I HAVEN'T EVEN GOTTEN STARTED YET!

I DON'T SEE LARDINE, GORKA!

TO HECK WITH LARDINE! IT'S DOWN TO US NOW...AND THAT'S ALL THAT COUNTS!

WE THREE WOULD BE AN INVICIBLE TEAM! TOGETHER WE COULD REVOLUTIONIZE BIBBUR-SI AND ALL THE OTHER MONSTER CITIES!

I NEED YOU...

...AND NOW YOU CANNOT REFUSE ME!

BUMP BUMP BUMP

ATCHOOO! ATCHOOO!

WHAT'S THE MATTER, ZICK?

IT'S THAT PRESENCE! I FEEL IT STRONGER THAN EVER...

...AND IT ISN'T MAGNA-CAT!

THERE'S ANOTHER MONSTER AROUND!

OH, YES... NOW I CAN FEEL IT TOO!

I'LL USE THE TONE ON IT!

HANG ON, ZICK, DON'T DO IT!

HEY YOU! COME OVER HERE! COME OUT OF THE FOG!

WHO ARE YOU TALKING TO?

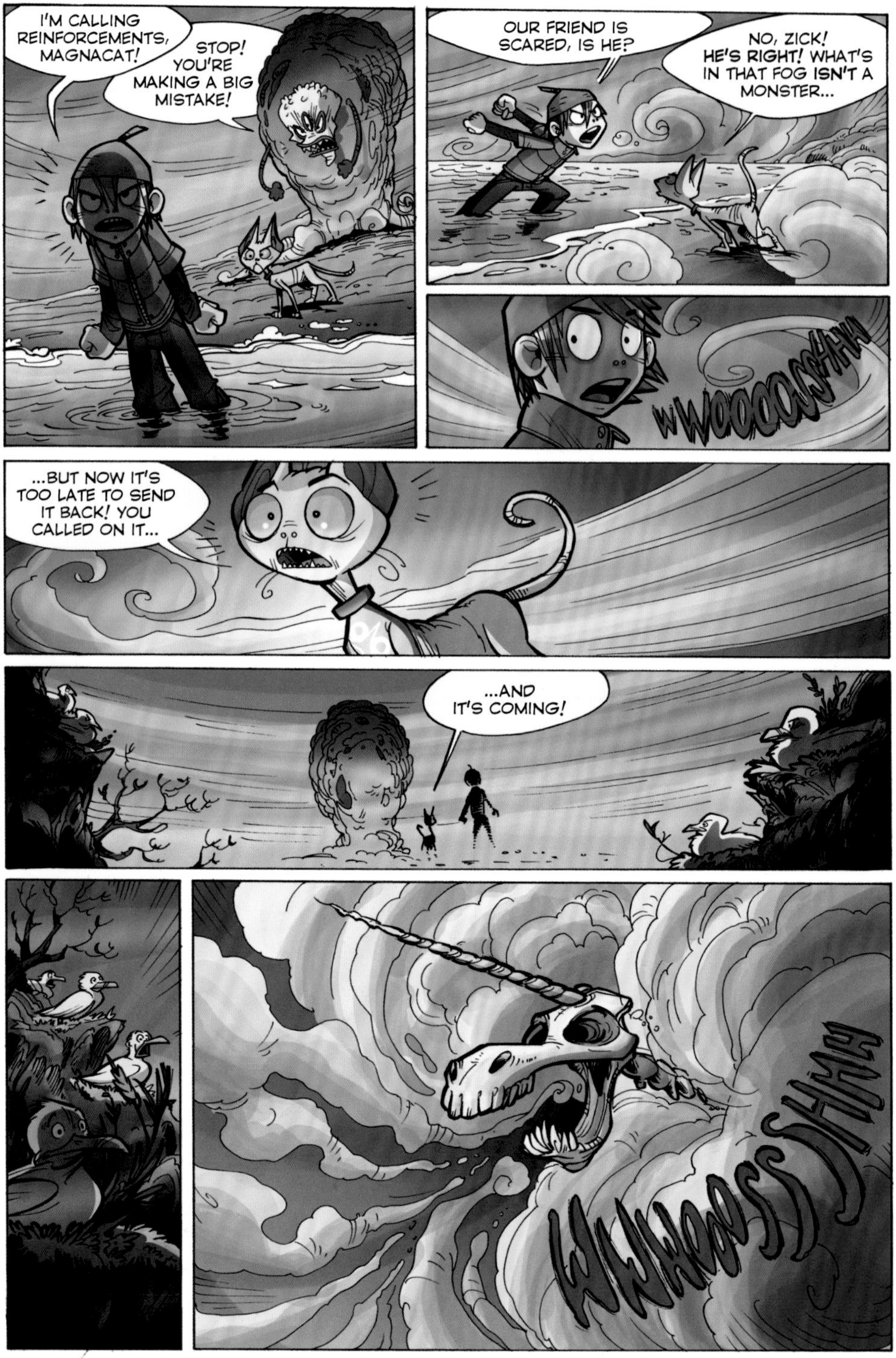
I'M CALLING REINFORCEMENTS, MAGNACAT!
STOP! YOU'RE MAKING A BIG MISTAKE!
OUR FRIEND IS SCARED, IS HE?
NO, ZICK! HE'S RIGHT! WHAT'S IN THAT FOG ISN'T A MONSTER...
WWOOOOSHHH
...BUT NOW IT'S TOO LATE TO SEND IT BACK! YOU CALLED ON IT...
...AND IT'S COMING!
WWHOOSSHHH

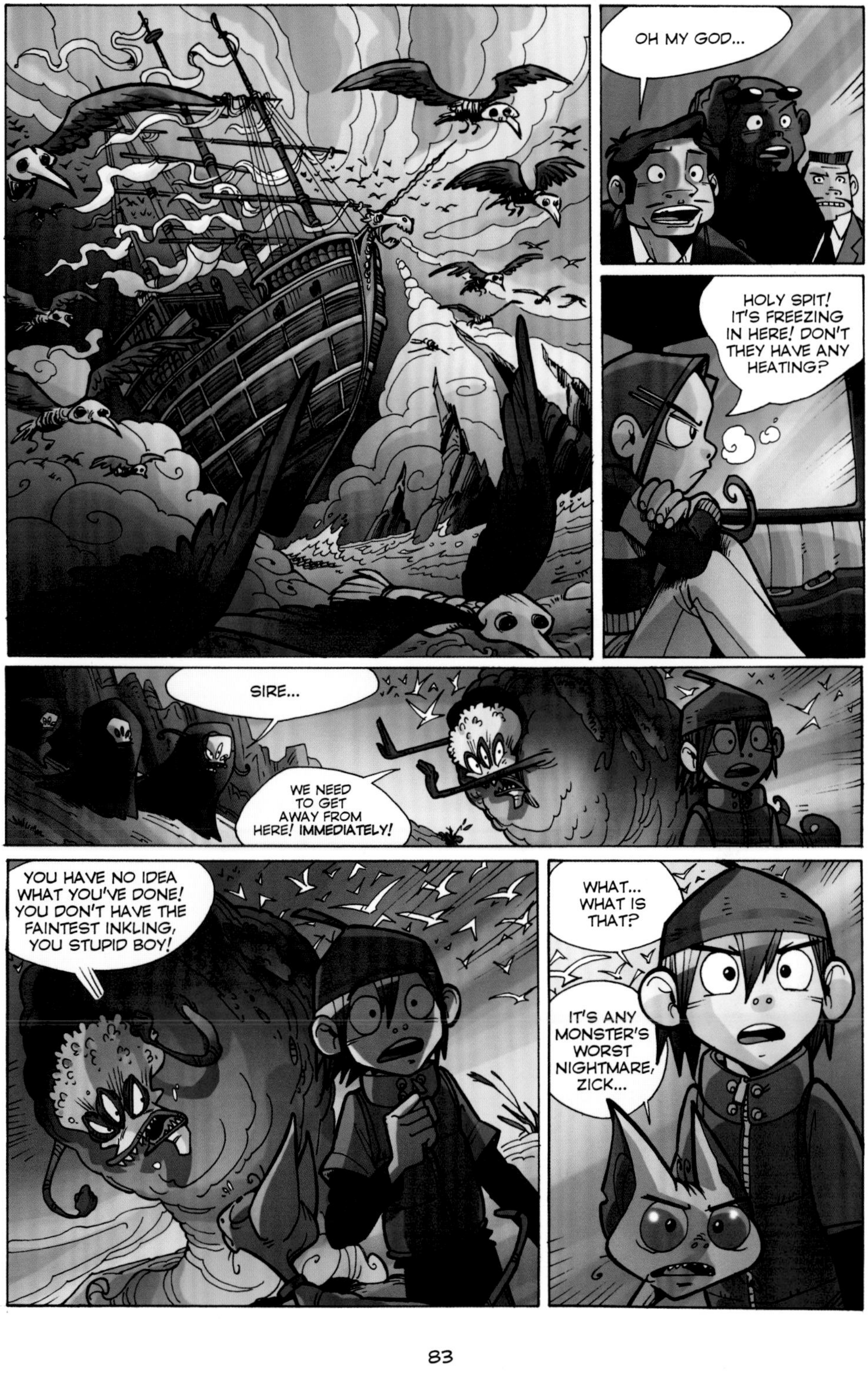
OH MY GOD...
HOLY SPIT! IT'S FREEZING IN HERE! DON'T THEY HAVE ANY HEATING?
SIRE...
WE NEED TO GET AWAY FROM HERE! IMMEDIATELY!
YOU HAVE NO IDEA WHAT YOU'VE DONE! YOU DON'T HAVE THE FAINTEST INKLING, YOU STUPID BOY!
WHAT... WHAT IS THAT?
IT'S ANY MONSTER'S WORST NIGHTMARE, ZICK...

...IT'S A BLACK PHANTOM!

WHO CALLED ME? WHO DARES TO GIVE ORDERS TO PIRATE CAPTAIN BRISTLEBEARD?

HIM!

HEY! THAT'S NOT TRUE!

A GORKA! AAAAH... IT'S BEEN CENTURIES SINCE I'VE TASTED MONSTER MEAT...

...NOW, GET OVER HERE! THERE'S ROOM FOR EVERYONE AT THE CAPTAIN'S TABLE!

WHAT ARE YOU WAITING FOR? STOP HIM! STOP HIM!

I THOUGHT THERE WERE ONLY GOOD GHOSTS!

YOU'RE THINKING OF WHITE SPIRITS, LIKE YOUR GRAND-PARENTS! THIS IS A BLACK PHAN-TOM...

THEY ARE DANGEROUS CREATURES! TORMENTED SOULS THAT TRY TO COME BACK TO LIFE...

...BUT THEY CAN ONLY DO SO BY EATING MONSTERS!

YAAAAAAAH!

HA...

THAT WAS A VERY POOR ATTACK, MY FRIEND!

URRRGH!

HARMPH!

AND NOW IT'S YOUR TURN!

AAAAAH!

MIGHTY MAGNACAT, HELP US!

HELP YOU? YOU'RE DOING SPLENDIDLY ON YOUR OWN! I COULDN'T DO A BETTER JOB OF GETTING EATEN MYSELF!

CHOMP! CHOMP! CHOMP!

BLECH! YUCK! SPIT!

IS THIS A JOKE? THESE CREATURES ARE ONLY HALF MONSTERS!

I NEED PROPER SUSTENANCE TO BECOME WHOLE AGAIN...TO BECOME SOLID...

STOP HIM, ZICK! TRY TO USE THE TONE OF THE TAMER AGAIN...

ERM... MR. BRISTLE-BEARD...?

MR. P THE PUNISHMENT FOR CALLING ME THAT IS TWENTY LASHES! WHAT DO YOU WANT?

I WANT YOU TO STOP! RIGHT NOW!

YOU'RE GOING TO HAVE TO DO BETTER THAN THAT TO STOP A HUNGRY GHOST! HA! HA!

I'VE BEEN WAITING THREE CENTURIES TO RETURN HOME! I'M THE CAPTAIN OF THE *UNICORN*...

I RAN HER ON MY OWN AFTER MY CREW LEFT ME...

...AND ONLY THE REEFS AND THE FOG COULD DRAG ME TO THE BOTTOM OF THE SEA!

ANF! GASP! KEEP TALKING, PHANTOM... KEEP TALKING!

SO DON'T EVEN TRY, BOY! A CAPTAIN DOESN'T TAKE ORDERS FROM ANYONE--I'VE ALREADY TOLD YOU THAT!

YES! I MADE IT! I'M SAFE!

OOF! FREE AT LAST!

KLANG

SLAM

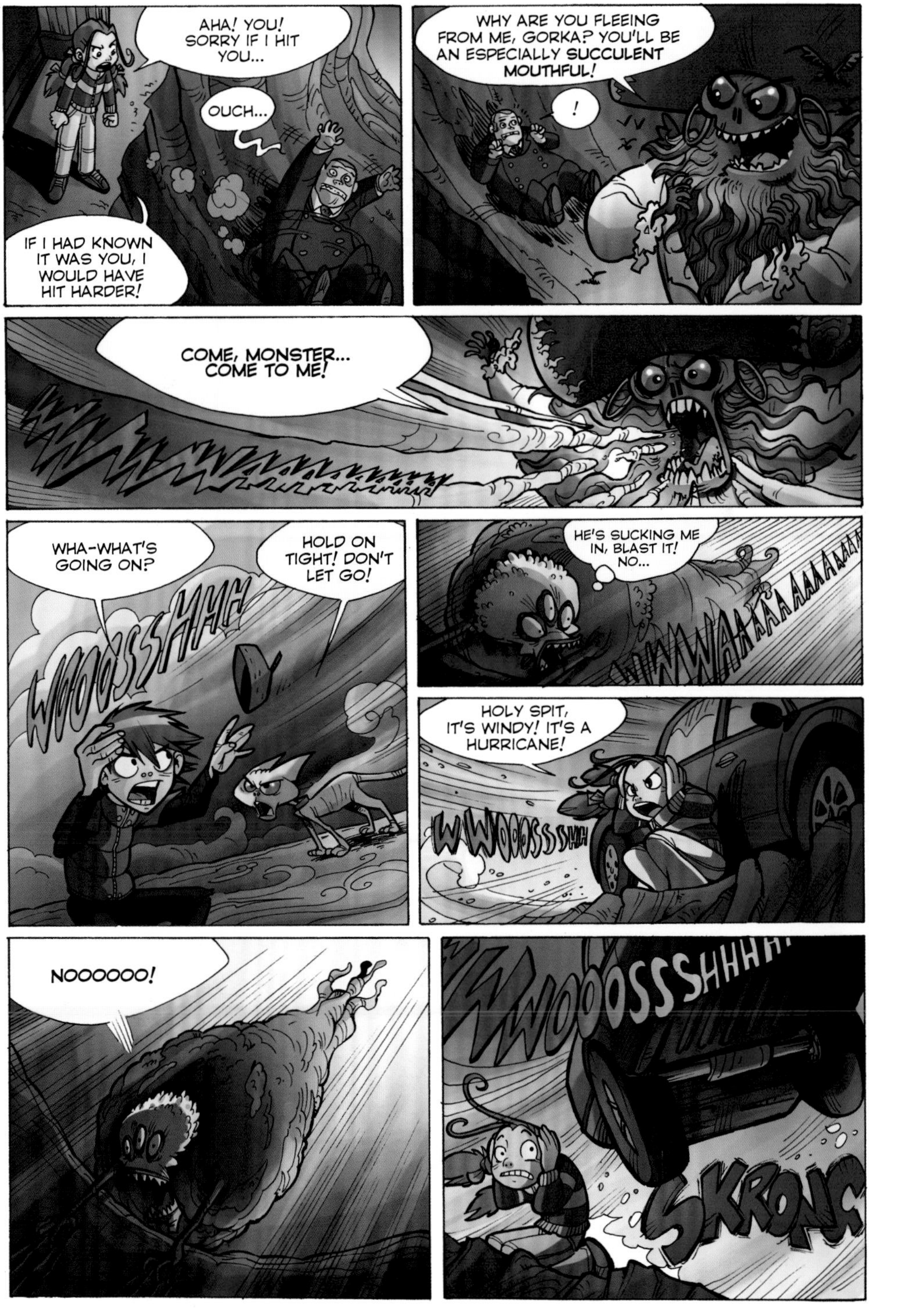
AHA! YOU! SORRY IF I HIT YOU...
OUCH...
IF I HAD KNOWN IT WAS YOU, I WOULD HAVE HIT HARDER!
WHY ARE YOU FLEEING FROM ME, GORKA? YOU'LL BE AN ESPECIALLY SUCCULENT MOUTHFUL!
!
COME, MONSTER... COME TO ME!
WHA-WHAT'S GOING ON?
HOLD ON TIGHT! DON'T LET GO!
WOOOSSHHH
HE'S SUCKING ME IN, BLAST IT! NO...
WWWAAAAAAAAAAAAAA
HOLY SPIT, IT'S WINDY! IT'S A HURRICANE!
WWOOOSSSHH
NOOOOOO!
WOOOSSSHHHH
SKRONG

KRA-BANG

AH!

WOOOSSHHH

AAAAAAAAHH

CHOMP CHOMP

BURP!

AND NOW, BACK TO US! I STILL SENSE THE SMELL OF MONSTERS!

CONCENTRATE, ZICK! DON'T LET HIM SCARE YOU...

...YOU CAN STOP HIM!

LEAVE MY CAT ALONE! YOU'VE ALREADY EATEN!

AND NOW... YOU...

...ARE...

...FULL!

HUH...

GOOD MOVE, BOY! AN EXCELLENT TRICK! I'M NO LONGER HUNGRY!

WELL, THEN... GO. BACK. TO. WHERE. YOU. CAME. FROM!

NOW YOU'RE EXPECTING TOO MUCH! I WON'T EAT ANYONE...BUT AS FOR GOING BACK, FORGET IT!

I'LL BE SEEING YOU AROUND.

THE CAPTAIN WILL RISE AGAIN!

IT DIDN'T WORK! I COULDN'T USE THE TONE LIKE I WANTED TO...

ON THE CONTRARY! NOW YOU KNOW HOW TO DIRECT IT! YOU ARE AMAZING!

OHHH...

ZICK!

ZICK! WHAT HAPPENED!

HE'S EXHAUSTED! TOO MUCH EXCITEMENT IN ONE GO!

BUT...YOU CAN TALK!

YEAH, BUT I'D RATHER YOU DIDN'T MAKE A BIG DEAL OUT OF IT...

ZICK! HE CAN TALK!

HE'S PERFECTLY AWARE OF THAT! NOW GET A GRIP AND LISTEN TO ME!

GET HELP FOR ZICK AND **THOSE BIG BABIES.** YOU NEED TO GET HIM HOME! **QUICKLY!**

I STILL HAVE SOMETHING TO SORT OUT IN THIS NEIGH-BOR-HOOD.

WOW.

OLDMILL VILLAGE.

ANOTHER CAPPUC-CINO?

NO THANK YOU, BOMBO! THAT WOULD BE THE FIFTH!

BUT CAPPUCCINO CURES EVERY ILLNESS! IT WORKS FOR ME!

IT SHOWS!

THAT'S ENOUGH NOW! DON'T ALL CROWD AROUND HIM. ZICK NEEDS TO REST.

BUT I'M NOT TIRED! AND YOU STILL HAVEN'T TOLD ME HOW YOU GOT THE **RABBIT** TO SPEAK!

OH, THAT...

EVER SINCE HE TANGLED WITH THE MONSTER POD, THAT POOR ANIMAL HASN'T BEEN THE SAME.

THAT'S BECAUSE THE CARNIVOROUS PLANT DIDN'T QUITE DIGEST THE RABBIT...

FLUFFY IS ONE OF US NOW! NOW CLOSE YOUR EYES AND SLEEP.

AND WHAT ABOUT PUNZO AND THE OTHERS?

THEY WENT BACK TO THEIR OLD LIVES!

ALL THE SLAVES HAVE BECOME FREE AGAIN.

MAGNACAT'S POWER DISAPPEARED WITH HIM.

MAGNACAT...

HE WOULD HAVE WON IF IT HADN'T BEEN FOR THE BLACK PHANTOM!

THE MEETING AT GLOOMY BAY BECAME A TRAP FOR HIM.

I GUESS HE WAS JUST UNLUCKY!

NO, ZICK! HE WAS CARELESS. BRISTLE-BEARD IS PROOF THAT BLACK PHANTOMS ARE ALL AROUND US...

...AND THERE ARE MORE OF THEM THAN WE THINK!

THOSE CREATURES ARE RESTLESS...AND THAT MAKES THEM DANGEROUS!

BLACK PHANTOMS ARE A THREAT FOR MONSTERS...

...BUT THEY CAN'T GET IN HERE.

I'D TAKE CARE OF THEM IF THEY TRIED!

WELL, ZICK...

MOM! DAD!

ONE MORE WORD AND YOU'RE IN DEEP TROUBLE!

GRETA, DEAREST... WE...

YOU PROMISED TO WATCH OVER ZICK!

YOU AGREED TO KEEP HIM AWAY FROM ALL THIS!

YOU PROMISED THAT HE WOULDN'T END UP LIKE HIS FATHER!

WE'RE SORRY, GRETA.

MOM...YOU...YOU CAN SEE THEM?

THEY WERE MY PARENTS, ZICK...

AND THEY STILL ARE. THEY ALWAYS WILL BE!

BUT WHY DIDN'T YOU EVER TELL ME?

YOU NEED TO BE CAREFUL, ZICK! YOU TOOK AN ENORMOUS RISK...

YOU DIDN'T ANSWER MY QUESTION!

I KNOW.

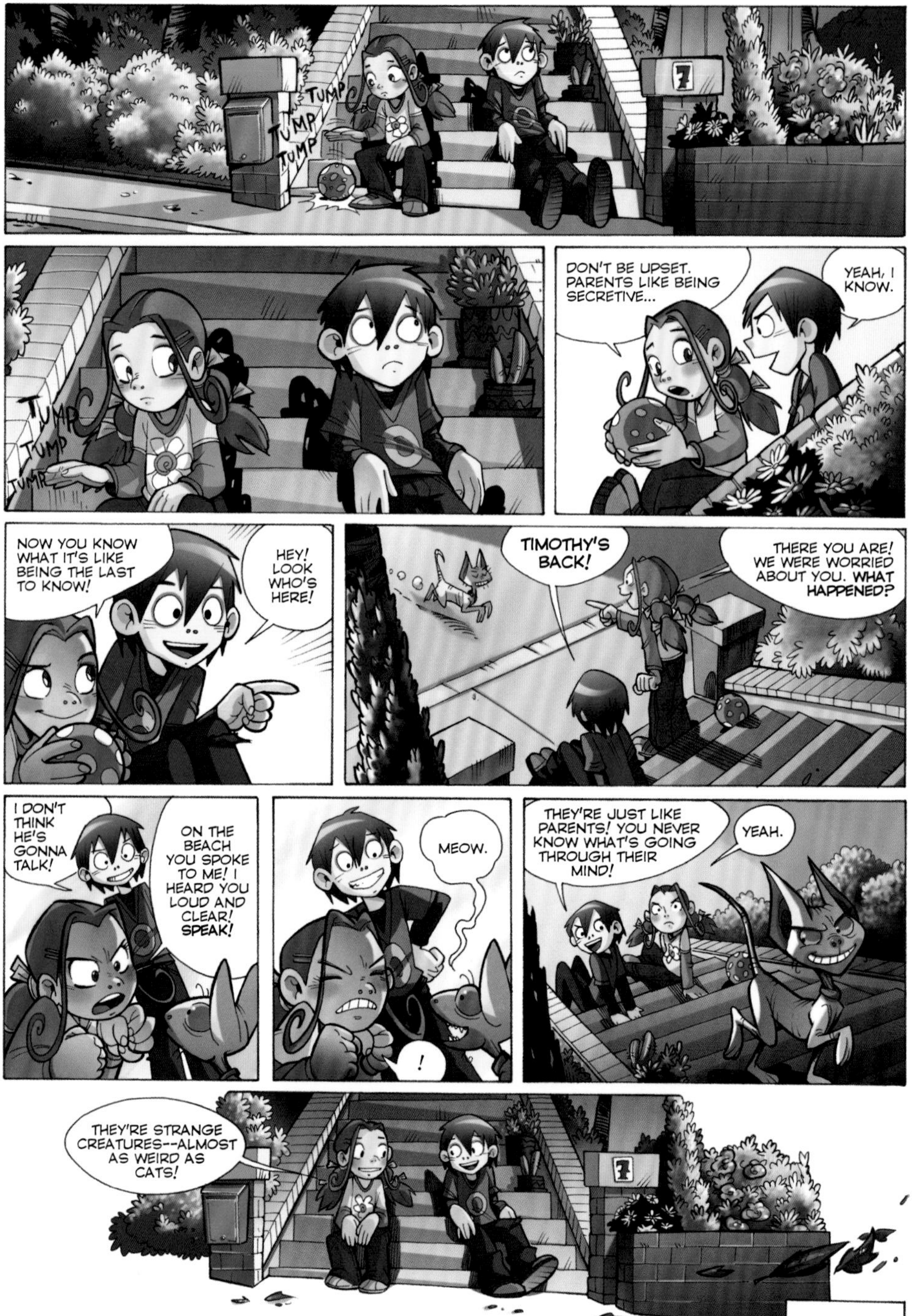
TUMP
TUMP
TUMP
TUMP
TUMP
TUMP
DON'T BE UPSET. PARENTS LIKE BEING SECRETIVE...
YEAH, I KNOW.
NOW YOU KNOW WHAT IT'S LIKE BEING THE LAST TO KNOW!
HEY! LOOK WHO'S HERE!
TIMOTHY'S BACK!
THERE YOU ARE! WE WERE WORRIED ABOUT YOU. WHAT HAPPENED?
I DON'T THINK HE'S GONNA TALK!
ON THE BEACH YOU SPOKE TO ME! I HEARD YOU LOUD AND CLEAR! SPEAK!
MEOW.
!
THEY'RE JUST LIKE PARENTS! YOU NEVER KNOW WHAT'S GOING THROUGH THEIR MIND!
YEAH.
THEY'RE STRANGE CREATURES--ALMOST AS WEIRD AS CATS!
THE END

An Imprint of Insight Editions
PO Box 3088
San Rafael, CA 94912
www.insightcomics.com

Find us on Facebook:
www.facebook.com/InsightEditionsComics

Follow us on Twitter:
@InsightComics

Follow us on Instagram:
Insight_Comics

First published by agreement with Tunué - www.tunue.com. All rights reserved.

Published in the United States in 2019 by Insight Editions. Originally published in Italian as part of
Monster Allergy Collection Vol. 1 and *Monster Allergy Collection Vol. 2* by Tunué, Italy, in 2016.

Library of Congress Cataloging-in-Publication Data available.

ISBN: 978-1-68383-541-7

Publisher: Raoul Goff
Associate Publisher: Vanessa Lopez
Executive Editor: Mark Irwin
Assistant Editor: Holly Fisher
Senior Production Editor: Elaine Ou
Design Support: Brooke McCullum
Production Manager: Sadie Crofts

ROOTS of PEACE   REPLANTED PAPER

Insight Editions, in association with Roots of Peace, will plant two trees for each tree used in the manufacturing of this book.
Roots of Peace is an internationally renowned humanitarian organization dedicated to eradicating land mines worldwide and converting
war-torn lands into productive farms and wildlife habitats. Roots of Peace will plant two million fruit and nut trees in Afghanistan and provide
farmers there with the skills and support necessary for sustainable land use.

Manufactured in China by Insight Editions

10 9 8 7 6 5 4 3 2 1